I0603200

LOSING PRIDE

MOUNT ROXBY SERIES: BOOK FIVE

AIMIE JENNISON

Contents

For the real Sassy Girl, who claimed Jared the first time she met him.
He was, and will always be, yours.

This book has been written using UK English and is set in Australia. I apologise if there are words or phrases you do not understand. Please feel free to contact me for further explanation, or to discuss the meaning of a particular phrase or word, via my email or any of my social media.

PANIC STATIONS

GRABBING the last bag of shopping, I follow Alyssa into the house that's slowly become home for me. It saddens me to think that once Alyssa is happy, and no longer needs an alpha's support to get through the day, things will change, and we'll most probably end up parting ways. She's become the sister I never had. Theo's pack safe house will once more lie empty until another pack member is in need of it and I'll have to look for a more permanent place to stay. With the connections that I've made here in Mount Roxby I'm certain my future home will be somewhere close by.

I don't plan on going back to the pride on a permanent basis. There are a number of strong lions back home who would make a great pride alpha. The pride can survive well without me and, maybe once my father steps down, a younger pride member not connected to our family line might bring a new lease of life into the pride.

I place the bags on the kitchen table and make quick work of putting the things away—all the while wondering what's happened to Alyssa. She usually insists on unpacking the shopping herself because I apparently put things in all the wrong places.

"Alyssa?" I call as I walk through the small house. Hearing the water running in the bathroom I knock on the door. "You okay in there, Lyss?"

The door opens and I step back to give Alyssa room to

pass. She grimaces. "I thought morning sickness was meant to stay away once you got through the first couple of months. It isn't meant to come back again."

"You've only got another couple of weeks left, be thankful you aren't going through a human length pregnancy," I remind her, following her through to the kitchen. Shifters tend to have a similar pregnancy length to their animal counterpart rather than the human nine months which is great for werewolves since they are forced to change with the moon's call, using alpha power to fight that is hard work and not always a guarantee, so the shorter the duration of pregnancy the better.

"Thank god, for small mercies. I'll take my five months over their nine any time." Sighing, she walks over to the pantry and looks it over, no doubt checking whether I've put things away to her standards.

I lean against the doorframe and watch her shuffle things around to her liking, grinning to myself knowing they'll only be messed up again when I use something because I never put them back from the exact spot I got them from. She fills the kettle and I stride over to her, tugging her gently away by her hips. "Lyss, go and sit down. You need to get all the rest you can before the baby arrives."

She turns and I catch sight of an eye roll. "I don't think making one cup of tea will kill me."

"Two," I correct as I pull down two cups. "And yes, it flaming would. Sit!"

She huffs before sitting on the bench at the table.

"Not there. The sofa." I gesture in the direction of the lounge to get my point across. "It's much comfier, you can even put your feet up."

Alyssa groans as she stands, rubbing her lower back. "Fine. I'm only moving so you'll shut up and give me some peace."

I laugh, knowing by her groan that she's lying. Her butt wouldn't have lasted very long on that hard wooden bench. "Sure, Lyss. Whatever you say."

She pokes out her tongue on the way out the room, causing me to laugh harder at her child like behaviour. It's good to see her being playful from time to time. It gives me hope that one day she'll be okay living in a world without her mate, Wesley.

I pour the hot water into the cups and swirl Alyssa's teabag with the spoon.

"*Jared!*"

Alyssa's terrified call has me running through the house. I find her next to the sofa, doubled over cradling her stomach, clearly in pain.

The eyes she turns on me are her wolf's. "There's something wrong."

"Try and stay calm. Your wolf can't help you or your baby right now." Her wolf energy floats over my skin as I stroke her back, hoping to give her some form of comfort. "Stand down," I address her wolf, making sure to push a little power towards her to make sure she does as she's told. I meant what I said; her wolf being in the forefront will only cause Alyssa and the baby more problems right now.

Alyssa's eyes return to her human eyes and she takes a few calming breaths as I continue to rub large circles over her back. "Thanks. She was making me panic and I couldn't focus on breathing."

"It's what I'm here for. How are you feeling now?"

She strokes a hand over her stomach and lowers herself onto the sofa. "Calmer. The pain's passed. I'm thinking it was maybe a Braxton Hicks."

I crouch before her and squeeze her knee. "I'm going to call the midwife, just so we can be sure everything is okay."

"I don't want to waste her time. Someone else might

need it more." Her worry is obvious in the way she pulls her lip between her teeth.

I stroke her leg before standing and pulling my phone out of my back pocket. "Alyssa, she said to call anytime. She'll be more than happy to come out even if it's just to ease your mind."

Scrolling through my phone I find Cassy's name and hit the call button. She answers within a couple of rings. "Jared, hi. Is Alyssa okay?"

"I'm fine. He's just over reacting."

I glare at Alyssa across the room. "You were in pain and your wolf was panicking. I'm not overreacting."

"I'm sure it's nothing to worry about but I think you guys should still come to the office and we'll do an ultrasound to check on the little one." Cassy's voice is calm, which does a lot to ease some of my worry.

"Thanks Cassy. We'll see you soon." Hanging up, I slip the phone into my pocket and grab Alyssa's handbag off the coffee table where she'd obviously left it on her way through to the bathroom. "You heard her. Come on."

"It's a waste of everyone's time," she grumbles, struggling to her feet.

Alyssa tugs her bag out of my hands and I follow her to the car. She leans heavily against the car door and releases a cry of pain. "Oh, god! I think this might be more than Braxton Hicks."

I stroke her back once again until she steps away. "You okay?"

She nods. "I think it's passed again."

"I'll get us there quickly, just to be safe. I don't fancy catching the baby in the back of the car." I open the door and wait for her to get in to be sure she isn't going to have another contraction.

Alyssa pushes on the door, not allowing me to close it.

"*Wait!* What if my waters break?" She glances down at the seat beneath her.

"That shit will clean. Don't you worry about it." I couldn't care less about the car cleaning. As an alpha I'm willing to do many things, but catching a baby is one I'd fucking really like to avoid.

———

WE ARRIVE at the medical practice in record time. I tried to stick to the speed limits but once Alyssa started panting again I decided flooring it was the best option. Once I get to the passenger side of the car Alyssa is already climbing out.

She doubles over in pain. "*Fuuuuck!*"

I scoop her up in my arms, deciding it's the quickest way to get her with the people she needs.

"Cassy Michaels. We need Cassy Michaels," I tell anyone who wants to listen.

A small brunette dashes out from behind the counter and runs down a corridor to her left. I follow her and watch her bang her fist on the last door on the right. "*Cassy!*" Not waiting to be invited in the brunette opens the door and Cassy jumps up from her desk.

Alyssa's fingernails dig into my shoulder as she lets out primal growl.

"It looks like the little one has decided it's time to make their entrance. Get her comfy over there." Cassy points to a medical bed, that looks anything but comfortable, before turning her attention to the brunette. "Can you grab everything we'll need for a premature birth?"

As I make a move to place Alyssa on the bed, she bats at my arm. "No. I need to be on my feet."

I glance across at Cassy, wondering if it's safe for her to be standing, since she'd gestured to the bed.

She nods. "Some women prefer a standing position. Gravity will give a helping hand that way."

Alyssa grips my shoulders to steady herself as I place her on her feet. "Thank you, Jared."

I place a gentle kiss to the top of her head and step back. "Anything for you, Lyss," I say, meaning every word—she's like family to me and there's nothing I wouldn't do for the woman.

She grips my hand not allowing me to get far. "I'm scared," she whispers. "I can't do this alone."

I squeeze her fingers in mine. "I'm not going anywhere. Okay?"

She pins me with her tear filled eyes. "I wish Wes was here."

"I know, sweetheart. I wish that too." I give her a small smile and rub her shoulder with my spare hand. "You'll just have to make do with me."

She wipes at a lone tear that's trailing down her cheek. "Well, I guess you'll do as a second choice." Her little grin gives me hope that she'll be strong enough to get through today without completely breaking. I couldn't have imagined her being this strong a few months back.

Alyssa starts to pace the room. "I think another contraction is coming." She braces her hands on the bed and I rub her back in a large circular motion. I allow my alpha energy to pulse over her skin, hoping it will make her feel safe and have a calming effect.

Once the contraction passes Cassy walks over. Completely dismissing me, her eyes fall on Alyssa. "Do you need to call your pack alpha?" Cassy is one of Misty's witch friends, who has made it clear throughout Alyssa's pregnancy that she doesn't approve of me looking after Alyssa rather than her pack mates, so her question doesn't surprise me in the slightest.

"Jared *is* my alpha now." Her words cause something inside me to shift and it takes a moment for me to feel what I know is a pride member bond.

"Alyssa—" Her name falls from my lips and I stop myself from saying the rest of the sentence, accepting her into my pride. If I accept her, her bond with the Mount Roxby Pack will be severed and even though she could technically go back to Theo and request to join again, I know she would never do that. They fact that I can feel a bond between us tells me she's serious about leaving them completely.

"I need this… I need…" Her broken sentence ends on a sob and I pull her into my arms.

"I know, Lyss. You heard me, I want to…but I need to call Theo first." She nods, and I release her, immediately pulling my phone from my pocket. I focus my eyes on Cassy. "I'll be back in two minutes."

Cassy steps up to Alyssa and places her arm over her shoulder. "Let's get you into a gown while Jared's out and we wait for the next contraction."

Striding towards the main doors of the building I hit call on Theo's name.

"Is it the baby? I felt her pain." The concern is clear in Theo's voice.

I run a hand over my head, suddenly wishing Alyssa hadn't taken so much off when she trimmed my hair the other day. "Yeah. It looks like it's coming a little early…" I leave my sentence hanging for a second while I try to formulate the next sentence.

Closing my eyes, I channel my lion to help centre me. He looks at the situation without my human emotions. "I'm accepting Alyssa into my pride." My voice sounds gruff with my lion so close to the surface, but I don't try to hide it. I need him to know I'm serious.

I hear Theo take a deep breath through the phone and

wait, knowing he'll respond in time. He needs to process this.

"Alyssa's pack bond has been getting weaker by the day. I figured this was coming." He sighs before going on, "I can't say I'm not sad about this outcome, but she's clearly made the decision to claim you as her new alpha and I'm not going to fight that."

The tension flows out of me hearing his words. "That's good to hear. I had every intention of accepting her claim, I just didn't want to do it behind your back."

"Just promise me you'll look after her."

"Always. I'll protect her and the baby with my life." The words fall out of my mouth without thought. It would be the same answer even if I weren't her alpha.

Hearing Alyssa's pain-filled cries through the building, I quickly end the call and shove my phone back into my pocket. It takes all my concentration to keep from using my supernatural speed to rush back into the room. I shove the door open with a little too much force, causing it to crash against the opposite wall, leaving a handle sized hole in the wall. "Shit!"

The small brunette woman from earlier follows me in, halting in the doorway as she looks around the room with wide eyes.

"Carrie-Ann, I need to talk to you outside."

I make quick work of getting across the room and to Alyssa. Noticing the fresh claw marks in the PVC of the bed, I give her a raised brow. "I think you need something less damageable to hold. Take my hand," I say, offering said hand to her.

She turns to face me, gripping my forearms in her hands and pinning me with her wolf's eyes. "If I don't survive this, promise me you'll do everything in your power to protect my baby."

"Alyssa Jones, you and your baby are mine to protect and

I will lay down my life before either of yours. We are Pride."
With my words a bond snaps in place between us and I can
feel her pain. I draw it away from her and into myself, as I've
heard other alphas can do.

Her shoulders sag and she drops her head against my
chest. "Thank you."

"We're going to get you through this, okay?" Hearing
that my voice is once again gruff alerts me to the fact that
my lion is close to the surface.

"Okay." Cassy's voice comes from the doorway and I
look over my shoulder in her direction, unable to hold back
the warning roar that escapes. "Holy shit! I think sending
everyone home and closing the practice was definitely a good
call."

Closing my eyes, I push down my lion enough to not
attack someone who is clearly here to help, yet not too far
that we can't keep pulling the pain from Alyssa. Opening my
eyes I apologise.

"Hey, it's to be expected. I'm not going to lie and say I
don't prefer these blue eyes to the golden ones you just
looked at me with." Her nervous laugh makes it clear I'd
scared her. "Alyssa, how are you doing? You look better than
you did a few minutes ago. I'm guessing it's something your
alpha is doing for you."

Alyssa nods. "Yes. I'm so glad he's here." She ends in a
grunt and grips my forearms tighter. "I'm feeling pressure
and want to push. But my waters haven't broken yet...
Shouldn't they have broken by now?" She lifts her eyes to
Cassy's and the terror I see in them as they flick past mine
worries me.

"Everyone is different, Alyssa. You're doing great. If you
want to push, do it." Cassy's words take away my worry and
I focus my attention back to Alyssa.

"Hear that, Lyss? You want to push, push."

"Oh god! Here it comes." Her fingernails break the skin on my arms as she bears down with a grunt. Cassy positions her hands between Alyssa's legs as she squats and I lower myself with Alyssa.

When the contraction is over Alyssa's grip on my arms eases.

"Okay, your waters are bulging and the baby's head is right there. If I pop your waters for you it should make everything happen much quicker and easier. Is that okay with you, Alyssa?"

Alyssa lifts her eyes to mine, uncertainty clear in her wide-eyed look.

"Quicker and easier sounds like a good idea. You look fucking exhausted, Lyss."

"Thanks Jared, you really know how to make a girl feel go—od." Her sentence finishes on a high pitch as a gush of fluids hits the floor beneath us, making me think Cassy must have taken advantage of Alyssa's distraction and popped the waters.

"Well, it looks like nature decided for you. So, on your next contraction give the biggest push you can."

Alyssa nods and starts to groan as Cassy looks at me excitedly. "Okay, here we go. Push, Alyssa. Push."

Alyssa groans as she once again bears down and we get lower and lower.

"Keep pushing. Bub's almost out."

Alyssa slumps and I catch her as Cassy moves off to the side, her attention focused on something in her hands.

A baby's cry fills the air and I let out a sigh of relief at the beautiful sound. Picking up Alyssa, I carry her over to a small leather sofa in the corner of the room and place her down gently.

"You've got a healthy baby boy," Cassy says from right behind me.

I step back giving her room and watch as she places the baby in Alyssa's open arms.

"He's beautiful…," the wonder in Alyssa's voice has me stepping closer to get a look at our new pride member.

"He's perfect," I whisper, not wanting to disturb the now quiet baby. I reach out and stroke his cheek gently with the back of my finger, feeling overwhelmed with emotions I can't quite separate. We'd spent the last few months focusing on keeping Alyssa calm so that this tiny little person could be. It's heartbreaking knowing that he'll never meet his daddy.

She lifts him slightly. "Do you want to hold him?"

"He's happy with his Mumma. I'll hold him later." I reach into my pocket and pull out my phone. "I'm going to go make some calls. I know a few people who will be happy to hear the good news."

Alyssa rubs a hand over her chest. "Do you think he'll be angry?"

Knowing she's thinking of Theo and the pack bonds she can no longer feel, I duck down so I'm at her eye level. "No, Lyss. He told me he knew it was coming, your bond had been fading." I stroke a finger over her cheek, wiping away the tear tracks. "He's sad, but he just wants what's best for you."

She gives me a small smile. "Well, I guess you should go make your calls." Her brow creases. "I don't think I'm ready to see them yet. I know I won't be able to feel them through the bonds anymore, but…"

"They'll understand, Lyss. Don't worry."

I give them both a quick kiss on the head and leave the room to make the calls. "I won't be long."

"We've got a few things to take care of here, so take your time," Cassy says as she makes her way over to Alyssa. Realising she's probably referring to something I wouldn't want to see I quicken my steps.

2

NEW ARRIVAL

I'VE BEEN PACING my office for what feels like hours and in reality must only be twenty minutes or so. The pain I felt with the loss of Alyssa's pack bond was more than I'd expected. Having felt it fade over the last few weeks I knew it was coming, her decision had been made. Although I'm pretty sure her decision to leave the pack was made all those months ago on the night of Wes's death, her bond only started fading as she got closer and felt safe with another alpha.

If I'd sent her away with someone else maybe she would have come back eventually, but that wouldn't have been good for her or the baby in the meantime. She needed an alpha, and Jared is one I would trust with any of my pack members. He has a big heart and would never use his alpha powers with bad intentions.

Bel's energy floats over my skin before the weight of her hand slides over my shoulder and across my chest as she steps around me. "I'm sorry it hurts." She places a gentle kiss against my breastbone. "You got as far as removing your shirt, do you not want to run after all?"

Placing my hands on her hips, I lift her until she hooks her legs around my waist and her arms around my neck. "I don't want to be away from the phone in case Jared calls again."

A mischievous glint sparkles in her eyes. "How about I

find another way to distract you?" She kisses her way across my cheek before tugging on my earlobe with her teeth.

I laugh. "You know, I think I like that idea."

"I can tell," she says as she squirms against the erection behind my fly.

I groan at the friction. "Darlin', if you keep that up I'll have you naked in seconds and I won't be gentle about it."

"Who said I wanted gentle?"

I crush my mouth against Bel's in a passionate kiss as I press her against the wall, blindly ripping the seams of her shirt with my fingers and not caring about it surviving the moment.

There's a chiming coming from my desk but all I want to do is enjoy what my mate is offering. My hands roam over her chest as I free her breasts from the bindings of her bra.

Bel tears her mouth away from mine. "Babe, you should get that. It could be Jared," she says breathlessly.

I rest my forehead against hers as we both catch our breath. "The cock blocker. I wish he'd given us another ten minutes."

She lets out a naughty sounding laugh. "Ten minutes wouldn't have been nearly long enough."

I press a kiss to her lips. "Yeah, well that's probably true." Pressing one more kiss to her lips, she unwraps her legs from around my waist and I lower her to the floor before striding over to my desk and picking up my ringing mobile, taking note of Jared's name flashing on the screen before accepting the call.

"How are they?"

"He's got the right amount of toes and fingers, so he's perfect," Jared says sounding stoked.

My heart constricts in my chest. "He?"

"Yeah."

"A little Wes," Bel states beside me a hand on her heart,

having heard Jared's side of the conversation clearly with her wolf's hearing. "Has she named him yet?"

"Not before I left to call you guys." There's a scuffing sound through the line, which makes me think Jared must be kicking at something on the floor. He most probably wants to end the call and get back to his pack members.

"How's Alyssa doing?" I ask, feeling how loaded that simple question is.

Jared takes a deep breath before talking. "I don't know how she felt before but she feels lighter than I'd expect… through the bond," he clarifies.

"Your connection probably has a lot to do with that. She's been floating, somewhat packless for months. To feel secure and part of a pack again will do wonders for her."

"In that case, we should have done this months ago." Anger is clear in the growl behind Jared's words.

I rub a hand over my face as Bel hugs my side. "She wasn't ready then. Tearing her fully away from the pack back then would have broken her completely. Even though she couldn't bear to be near us, she needed the bond she'd been used to."

"She's getting anxious. I need to go," he says hurriedly, obviously feeling something through the bond.

My heart constricts knowing I was missing that now, something I'd never feel with Alyssa again. "Go, we'll chat later," I say.

"Send her our love and let us know when she feels up to visitors," Bel calls out.

"Sure thing," is all we hear before the line goes dead and I place my mobile back on the desk.

I stare at the phone as Bel's hands slide up my chest and around my neck. My skin ripples as my wolf tries to get out.

"Let's go for a run before we finish what we started earlier," Bel suggests. "Last one to the creek gets to take charge in the bedroom."

Bel disappears from before me with a pop and I laugh when she reappears outside the office window, quickly stripping out of her clothes.

"That's cheating, if you win it's null and void."

She looks at me with a raised brow. "You're the alpha, I should at least get a head start." She pokes out her tongue before running to the tree line and shifting in mid-air.

I take my time strolling out of the house, quite liking the idea of letting Bel take charge. I love it when she gets all bossy.

3

ENTERTAIN YOUR LIONESS

JARED

IT'S BEEN six weeks since Alyssa had the baby and I can't even remember what it was like before Little Lee arrived. Taking the bottle out of Lee's mouth, and holding his tiny chin in my hand as my forearm supports his body, I gently pat his back with my other hand, burping him. Lee is such a windy baby; the burps he comes out with are award worthy.

I listen through the small house I've been sharing with Alyssa since that terrible night her world fell apart and smile as I hear her soft snores. The poor thing hardly ever sleeps. I had to use my alpha power to order her to sleep today. Losing Wes would have killed her if she hadn't been pregnant; Lee is the only thing that's kept her going this last six months. In saying that, she's been living like a zombie, which is barely living at all…more like just existing. If I have to use a bit of my alpha power to help her along, I will.

I'm not the only one using alpha power on her. She still won't see the pack, so Theo ordered her to call him on a daily basis—he may not be her alpha anymore but he cares about her and will never walk completely away from her—so she does, grudgingly. Drastic times calls for drastic measures.

Well burped, I put Lee back in the crook of my arm and give him the last of his bottle. A loud banging on the door has me jumping off the sofa and opening the door.

"Fucking hell, could you bang any louder?" I snap at the female on the doorstep, a female I recognise from Quilpie.

Lee grumbles and I lay him on the tea towel that's laid over my bare shoulder and pat him gently on the back. I catch the female eyeing my naked chest with appreciation but I don't acknowledge it. We hardly ever get visitors, not since Alyssa can't handle seeing any of the wolves. So I didn't really worry when Lee spat up some milk on my t-shirt and I pulled it off. I'm wishing I had now.

"Jared?" Alyssa calls through the house, and the sleep in her voice doesn't hide the concern.

I hear the rustle of sheets and shout back. "It's okay, Lyss. Go back to sleep!" She's only had half an hour. I'm not letting her get up yet.

Alyssa growls in return but I can hear the sheets rustle again as she settles back down in the bed, giving in to my order.

"She's not happy about that order," the female before me says with a laugh.

I arch a brow at her, wondering what the fuck she's doing at my door.

"Theo Wilson told me I could find you here. Your dad is going to be pissed that you have a cub he knows nothing about," she states. The bitter tone in her voice makes me think my father wouldn't be the only one pissed about that.

Lee chooses that moment to shift in my hold. His hands turning to paws, his claws scratching at my shoulders as he tries to grip on. "He's not mine," I clarify, unnecessarily.

"I can see that," she says, watching me shift the pup around in my arms trying to stop his sharp little claws from drawing blood.

I inhale and catch the scent of lion. A scent that should make me feel homesick but it only solidifies my need to stay away from Quilpie and the lions I once thought of as family. *My pride.* "You've found me, so what can I do for you?"

She glares at me. "I want to be here just as much as you

want me here, but Grigori sent me and told me not to return without you."

I turn my back on her. "You'll have a long wait," I say as I push the door to. She puts her foot in the way, effectively stopping me from closing it, and I turn my eyes back on her.

"He needs your help, Jared." She looks at me with sad, pleading eyes. "At least let me explain the situation before you send me away."

I've never been able to say no to pleading eyes. I sigh as I look at my watch. "Fine. You better come in." I walk into the lounge and place a sleeping pup in his Moses basket and watch as he shifts back to human. I tighten his nappy tabs, as they always seem to loosen when he shifts, before turning to face the lioness who has taken a seat on the sofa. "Saskia, you are one of the last people I expected him to send."

She lifts a brow and grins, her sassy self shining bright just like I remember. "Really? Your father was always going to try to tempt you with a female and I pulled the short straw."

Her explanation made no sense. I was never one chasing after the girls. The only girl I showed any interest in was Bel and my initial interest in her was platonic, the alpha in me wanted to protect her. "My father still doesn't understand me."

Clearly guessing my thought process Saskia defends him. "After hearing Bel had mated with the local alpha he thought you might be interested in other women. I guess he was right because you're living with one."

"Jared is a true alpha, he looks after those in need regardless of their sex," Alyssa states, entering the room from the hallway to my left.

I glance at my watch. "You haven't had long."

She yawns. "I couldn't get back to sleep." I lift a brow but don't argue.

Saskia looks at Alyssa guiltily as she takes in her tired and fragile appearance. "I'm sorry, I should have been quieter."

Alyssa waves a hand in dismissal. "It's fine. I don't find sleep at the best of times, I'm not used to an empty bed." I watch as she gulps and blinks back the tears. "Tea? Coffee? I know Jared wouldn't have offered. He's a terrible host."

Saskia smiles warmly. "A tea would be great."

Alyssa walks into the kitchen, no doubt grateful for the few minutes to gather herself. She's only just started to manage getting through a day with just a teary moment or two. There was a point when she was in constant tears. Her anger hasn't eased up, but I don't think it ever will. At times I wonder if the hormone change since having Lee has made her take a step back in the healing process, then I worry if it's the change from pack to pride, maybe I'm not enough for her. Theo assures me it's not that, but having never had my own pride before I worry I'm not doing things right.

I turn to look at Saskia as I take a seat on the armchair. "So, what's happening in Quilpie? Why am I needed?"

"There's a group of Cleaners trying to kill us off," she states blandly, like it's nothing. Cleaners are a group of humans, born and bred for one thing and one thing alone—to eradicate the existence of supernatural beings, whether it be shifters, vampires or even witches. They don't care about the age or sex of their victims. All they care about is whether we're supernatural or not.

"The ones that attacked not long after I left?" I ask, remembering a phone call from Dad months ago.

My phone vibrated in the arse pocket of my jeans. I contemplated ignoring it, but I'd had a niggling in my gut since the night before that something somewhere wasn't right, I just knew it. I pulled it out and, without looking at the screen, hit answer.

"Hello," I shouted into the phone as I made my way out of Misty's. I would've had no problem hearing the caller over the noise of

the crowded bar but I knew whoever it was on the other end would've had trouble hearing me, whether they were a shifter or not.

"Jared, is that you?" My father asked.

"Hang on, I'm just going outside," I said, not knowing whether he'd heard me or not, as I walked through the emergency exit and into the alley behind the bar. The door closed, and the noise was locked behind Misty's magical wards. "Dad, is everything okay? I have a strange gut feeling that I don't like."

"That's why I'm calling. There's a group of Cleaners who attacked the pride during last night's hunt. We lost three males - Rico, Brian and Malone."

"The trouble causers then? I think the Cleaners did you a favour," I replied, knowing those three won't be missed by many.

"Well, I wasn't going to say that out loud—"

"Grigori, Jared… Don't be so unsympathetic. Those males were someones' sons," Mum called down the phone, obviously hearing me with her lioness's advanced hearing.

We both apologised at the same time.

"Sorry Mum."

"Sorry Dear."

Kicking an empty bottle across the alley, I listened to Dad grovel some more on the other end of the line. The sudden crash caused a cat to scatter from behind a dumpster.

"Jared, what was that?" My dad asked, the concern in his voice came through the phone loud and clear.

"Nothing, it was just a cat I scared. Do you need me to come home?" I asked, getting back on subject.

I could hear Mum's voice in the background but she wasn't speaking loud enough for me to discern the words.

"No, stay where you are for now. We can handle things here. It shouldn't be too hard to track down the Cleaners and end them before they try again. We managed to cut their number down significantly last night even though we'd been surprised by the attack. If there is a next time, we'll be ready for them."

Relief from his words ran through me and I felt the tension in my shoulders dissipating. "You'll tell me if you need me won't you? The pride comes first." I couldn't say the words with as much meaning as I once would have. I may be the next in line to lead the pride but it hasn't felt like my home for a long time. The lions have acted superior to other species of shifters for as long as I can remember, and that's not who I am or what I believe in.

When my grandfather was alpha, our hunts consisted of us leaving our territory to hunt and kill other shifters'—children were always protected, but adults were fair game. When my father took over and changed our prey to regular animals on our own land it almost caused a mutiny. His explanations of the land being overrun with animals helped calm things down. I don't know what he was thinking when he allowed Jack and Lillian to foster Rosabel, an orphaned werewolf. You didn't need to be psychic to know her life would be in danger the moment she was old enough to duel.

"Of course I will, Son." Dad's voice pulled me out of my thoughts. "Make sure you call your mother more, she worries about you being in that town."

I laughed. "She always worries."

"I'm your mother, it's my job to worry," she called out in the background.

"Take care of yourself." Dad disconnected the call after his parting words.

It's astonishing to think he hasn't eradicated them already.

She sighs. "Yeah, those will be the ones." She looks down as she picks at her blue nail varnish. I don't remember her being the nail varnish type. "They keep attacking at our weakest moments and our weakest pack members. The latest attack was when Rebecca Mason had her cubs, twins. They were barely a day old when the Cleaners executed the whole family."

I struggle to hold the anger at my father back. "Why

wasn't he hunting the fuckers down?" I snap, causing Lee to cry in his basket. I quickly walk over and gently rock it. "Shhh, it's alright buddy."

"They're good at covering their tracks, and his best tracker left town," Saskia says sadly.

"He needs you!" Alyssa comes in repeating Saskia's words from earlier. She hands a cup to Saskia and places another on the table in front of the seat on the sofa where I usually sit.

"Where's yours?" I ask, lifting up a brow.

She sighs. "Fine." She picks up my cup and downs it in one. "Happy now?" she says before taking my seat and putting her feet up on the table.

"I guess I asked for that." I take a seat in the armchair again. "I'm needed here. Can't he petition one of the other packs for help?" The second the sentence leaves my mouth I know it's a stupid suggestion for our pride.

Saskia laughs. "Have you forgotten what our pride is like? We don't mix well with other species."

"Maybe that's why the bounty hunters are preying on you," Alyssa suggests before focusing on me. "Your pride needs you, Jared, you have to go."

"*You're* my pride now Lyss." I get up and pace the room, feeling myself being torn in two. That pride is no longer mine, but I still feel the pull and responsibility to help them. I'm still bonded with them. The bonds may be faint now but they are still there. Alyssa needs me here though, she can't be left on her own. "I need to speak to Theo," I say, walking out of the house and into the tiny backyard. I pull out my phone and hit dial on Theo's number. It only rings twice before he picks up.

"Jared. I guess the pretty little lioness found you." I can picture the grin he's probably wearing.

"Yeah, thanks for the warning, mate. My dad needs me

to track some bounty hunters down, they seem to be picking off pride members left, right and centre." I pace the yard knowing I'm going to be wearing a track in the grass and not caring one bit. It's one of the pack's safe houses. Theo can get a gardener in to fix it. It serves him right for not warning me about Saskia.

"I guessed he was asking for you to go back. Send a pretty female to lure you home. It's a shame he doesn't know you well." He laughs. "I would've sent an injured pride member, someone the bounty hunters had done a good job on."

"Yeah, I'd be halfway home already," I admit, unimpressed that the alpha wolf can read me so well. "I don't want to leave Lyss and Lee."

I hear Theo sigh into the phone. "If it wasn't your pride I'd suggest you take her with you, but I know they don't like outsiders. You can't track the bounty hunters and protect Alyssa and Lee from your pride at the same time."

I pause, staring into the distance and trying to think of some solution that means I can help everyone who needs me. "I'm not leaving Alyssa alone, and she's not ready to be in the vicinity of a wolf." It's the only thing I can think about.

"Let me make some calls. Go and entertain your lioness. I'll get back to you soon." Theo says before hanging up.

Entertain my lioness? She can entertain her flaming self!

4

HOME OR AWAY

SILENCE FILLS the car as Saskia drives us into town in the car she'd left at the airport. I can't stop thinking about Alyssa and Lee, and how they'll be without me. I'm their alpha now and it's taking everything in me to leave my pride members back in Mount Roxby when I know they need me. Theo insisted he'll sort out their protection, but Alyssa hasn't been able to be in the vicinity of another wolf so I can't see how he'll manage. I'd left her with Theo's sister, Ruby, who I know will do her best; but being newly mated, and a vampire, means she won't be with Alyssa twenty-four seven like I've been.

My phone lets out a shrill ring and I quickly pull it out of my pocket. Seeing Ruby's number I can't keep the worry out of my voice. "Ruby, is everything okay?"

"Everything is fine. I'm just checking you landed safely. You aren't the only one that's allowed to worry, you know?" She chuckles down the line and, hearing the sound, I relax for the first time since leaving the house.

"Yeah, whatever." I laugh before sobering quickly. "How is she?"

"*She* is fine," Alyssa's voice says in the background. "I'm not as big a wreck as I once was, okay?" Lee's cries come through the phone and I suddenly realise I miss my little man. "Just make sure you come back in one piece." Hearing

Lee's cries fade as a door closes I gather Alyssa has taken him into another room.

"How is she really?"

Ruby lowers her voice, knowing doors aren't exactly sound proof for us supernatural beings. "Honestly Jared, she's good. She's not singing and dancing but… she's healing and you've helped her do that."

I run a hand through my hair. "I know but I don't like to think of her alone." I can see Saskia's frown out the corner of my eyes as she listens to the conversation.

"She's not alone. I'm watching over her for now and Theo has someone else from out of town arriving tomorrow."

I feel a rumbling growl escape from deep in my throat. I don't like the idea of a stranger stepping into my shoes. Realistically I know Theo wouldn't let anyone near Alyssa and Lee unless he trusted them one hundred percent, but I can't help but worry. "Make sure she rings if she needs me. No matter what time it is. Same goes for you, okay?"

"I promise." The sincerity in her voice brings a small smile to my face. "Now, you need to listen to what Alyssa said and come back in one piece because you have a number of people here who will miss you if you don't."

"I'll be careful." I quickly end the call before she says anything else that could make me feel more emotional than I already am. I really don't want to have to fight tears in front of Saskia. I clear my throat as I put the phone back in my pocket.

Saskia flicks her eyes from the road, to me, and back again. "You seem to have your own little pride back in Mount Roxby. I don't think we'll be getting you back here; not on a permanent basis like your father is hoping anyway."

I think about her words while I look around as we pull into town, taking in the familiar houses and few pride members I can see on the streets going about their business. I can feel deep down that this place isn't my home anymore but I daren't admit it out loud, not yet.

Saskia pulls to a stop outside my parent's house, stopping the engine with a turn of the key. Taking a deep breath I reach for the handle. Saskia's hand on my forearm stops me from opening the door. "Wait!" I look down at her hand on my arm before turning to face her. "If the pride really needed you, you would come back, wouldn't you?" She shakes her head. "Forget I just asked that." I can feel her concern for the pride's welfare through the faint pride bonds.

I reach out, taking her hand in mine. "This pride will always be a part of me, even when my bonds fade completely. I may be needed more elsewhere right now, but look where I am. I'm here. I will come when I'm needed. Always." She watches my thumb moving over her knuckles for a second before nodding, obviously satisfied with my answer.

I open the door and exit the car pulling my backpack over my shoulder as Saskia turns the engine over. I listen to her drive off as I look up the path to my childhood home. The door opens and Mum barrels towards me. I brace myself, ready for the collision, knowing I'll be knocked over if I don't.

"Jared!" she calls as she hits me at full force. "I'm so glad to see you!"

"I miss you too, Mum," I say with a chuckle. I wrap my arms around her and enjoy the love I can feel pouring through the bonds.

"Elaine?…Darling?" Hearing the worry in my dad's voice has me releasing Mum.

She holds me at arms' length and shouts over her shoulder. "I'm out here, Grig. Jared's home." She rakes her eyes over my face. "You look well. Someone must be feeding you."

"I'm feeding me, Mum. I am a big boy now, you know." I shake my head. Did she really think I wouldn't be eating?

My father is down the path within seconds. "She's right. You look much better than I'd imagined you to look." He pulls me against his body, clapping me on the back. "Especially after being away from the pride for so long. It's good to see you, Son." He steps back and glances to the road. "Where's Saskia?"

I look up the road towards where I remember her house to be, a few streets away. "Home, I guess."

"I know she wasn't happy with me sending her but I thought she would have at least come in for a minute, even just to say hello to your mother." Placing a hand on the base of my mum's back, he guides her up to the house and I follow behind, hitching my bag higher on my shoulder after it dropped during the family hugs.

"What am I going to feed you? I better go and start something for dinner." The panic in my mum's voice has me tugging her hand to stop her running off.

"Mum, don't put yourself out. I can go to the chippy down the road once I've had a chat with Dad." My mouth salivates just mentioning the fish and chip shop. Mount Roxby has some decent takeaways, but their fish and chips aren't as good as ours here in Quilpie.

"Nope, you need a good home cooked meal," she states while walking into the kitchen.

Dad and I both shake our heads. "Pick your battles, Son." Dad's familiar phrase reminds me of when I was younger and I'd come home complaining about how Rosabel was driving me insane. He always told me to pick my battles, stating that it's easier to let the women win.

I follow him into his office with a smile on my face. The

room doesn't look any different to the last time I was in here, telling him I was leaving to go after Rosabel. He was fuming but he knew I needed to go. I needed to follow Bel to see what fate had in store for us. It turns out we were meant for different paths and I'm okay with that. She's happy with Theo and I know now no matter how much I may have wished it would be different; I could never give her what he has. *A true mate.*

Forgetting the past, I walk across the room and sit on the green leather two-seater sofa positioned against the wall opposite his desk.

Dad spins his chair around, sitting in it so he's facing me. "So, tell me about this woman and cub you have living with you." My eyes flick up from his walnut desk and lock on his. How does he know about that? Saskia told me he didn't know when she arrived. Had she called him and filled him in on everything about Mount Roxby after she'd arrived? "Don't be upset with Saskia. She was following orders," Dad states having guessed my thoughts. "Begrudgingly, I might add."

I sigh, letting my annoyance at Saskia drain away. "What do you want to know? It sounds like you know plenty."

"Jared, you know Saskia well enough to know if she's mad at you she'll tell you as little as she can get away with. I'd overlooked that when I'd initially set my order." Although his words sounded stern, the slight lift of his lips in a small smile tells me he's impressed with her efforts.

"Yes, I remember. Sassy Saskia was what I used to call her," I admit, causing Dad to throw his head back with a laugh. "Alyssa is the wolf I've been living with. And Lee he… spits up a lot." I feel my mouth lift into a smile as I say their names. They may not be mine, but they are family to me.

"Is the cub yours?"

Dad's question shocks me and the disapproval in his

voice turns my smile into a frown. "And if he is? Are you disappointed because his mother is a wolf?" My hands are shaking on my lap as they form fists.

"Calm down, Son. I would never think like that. The rest of the pride may, but your mother and I would never be disappointed about something like that. We would be disappointed that you hadn't told us when you were expecting him." The hurt in his voice causes me to kick myself. Of course that would be why he'd be disappointed—I'm his only child, they'd want to know if they had their first grandchild on the way.

"He's not mine," I say quickly, hoping to ease the hurt. "Alyssa lost her mate early in the pregnancy. It was a scary few months trying to keep her calm through her grief so she wouldn't lose the pup too."

"You helped her through that?" Dad's wide eyes tell me he's surprised at the fact. He shouldn't be, he should know I'd help anyone that needs it.

"Of course I did. Why wouldn't—"

"You misunderstand me." His words cut me off. "I was surprised that her pack and alpha allowed you to do that."

"Sorry, I'm a little defensive. I don't like being away from them," I say with a small shrug. "Theo, her alpha, had no choice because she couldn't bear to be near another wolf, it reminded her of her lost mate. She still can't be near them, in fact… She claimed me as her Alpha. That's why I'm so worried about having left them." I tense, waiting for his reaction to hearing I've claimed new pride members.

He leans forward in his chair and pats my knee. "I won't keep you away from your little pride long, so don't be worrying." I breathe a sigh of relief at his words as he sits back in his chair and steeples his fingers under his chin. His typical thinking pose. "Her previous alpha will have someone looking out for her while you are gone, won't he?"

"Yes, Dad. Actually his sister is staying with her for now." Seeing the frown on his face I answer the question I know he's probably going to ask. "No, she isn't a wolf. In fact, she's a vampire." I hold my breath waiting for his reaction. Shifters and vampires have usually been enemies so I'm pretty sure he'll have something to say about the two being so closely connected.

"A vampire being part of a werewolf pack. That's… interesting," he says, nodding his head at the thought.

"Yes, and just to make it more interesting she's mated to one of the pack enforcers." I shrug, dismissing that conversation and quickly jumping on to the next. "So, fill me in on what's been happening here."

Dad stands, pushing his chair under his desk as he turns to look at the darkening view out the window. I close my eyes, seeing the view in my mind. The red dirt scattered with shrubs and bush right up to the dry creek bed at the end of the property. There's probably a lion or two wandering around or heading home, their golden fur stained red from lying in the dirt sunbathing all day long.

"There's a unit of Cleaners out there somewhere, fucking hunting us down." My eyes pop open with his words. My father never swears. "Picking off our weakest members one at a time." He lets out a roar and I know that he's fuming.

"Why haven't you hunted them down yet?" I ask, not really thinking about my words.

He spins around and his anger hits me, eliciting a hiss of pain from my mouth. "Do you not think I've tried? I don't know what they are using to hide themselves but we can't track them. They leave no scent, no tracks, *not a damn thing!*" He spins back around to peer out the window again. "Calling you in was a last resort. I've known for a long time our pride isn't the place for you." I open my mouth to speak but he shakes his head. "No, let me finish. I know you love the pride and care for every one of its members' wellbeing. If anything happens to me I know you'll come straight back to take control if there isn't anyone here that you deem suitable for the job."

I nod my head in agreement, even though I know he can't see me. Maybe he does know me after all.

"You have your little pride in Mount Roxby, and I have a feeling it will be getting bigger in time." He turns and meets my eyes "You've found your place in the world and both your mother and I are extremely proud of you."

Something inside me melts away as another part of me can't believe my ears. "You aren't disappointed?" I run a hand through my hair and suddenly realise it's gotten long since last time it was cut, before Lee's birth.

"No, Son. There is nothing you could do that disappoints me. You don't have it in you."

I can feel his pride pouring off him and can't help but straighten my shoulders because of it. Maybe my father will accept my choices in life down the line.

The door opens and mum walks in. "He's right." She takes a seat beside me and leans into my side. "We love you, Jared."

I quickly place my arm over her shoulders and hug her in closer. "I love you too, Mum." My eyes connect with Dad's and he winks at me as I give him a slight nod of the head. Our versions of *'I love you'*.

5

DISTURBED PRIDE

BOOM. Boom. Boom.

Jumping out of bed, I yank my door open wide and storm towards the front door, where the banging's coming from. I glance at the clock in the hall, seeing it's only two in the morning. Immediately my annoyance falls away. Nobody would disturb Dad at this time of night without good reason. Something has to be wrong.

I open the door to find Stephanie, one of the teenagers of the pride, staring at me, eyes wide in terror.

"*Cleaners!* Cleaners are attacking Pete and Rosie's place. Beth told me to come for you… your Dad… I don't..."

Seeing her stumbling over her words, I reach out and pull her into a hug. "You did good, Steph."

I hear Dad's thunderous steps behind me.

"What's happening?" Mum's voice calls from behind him.

Dad turns. "I told you to wait in the bedroom until I knew it was safe."

I thrust Stephanie towards my mum and dad. "Cleaners are attacking," I say, before running out the door wearing nothing but the sweats I'd slept in.

Saskia falls into step beside me as I get closer to Pete and Rosie's house. "What the fuck are you doing here?"

"The same thing as you," she mutters, her angry tone alerting me not to argue with her.

I shouldn't argue anyway. If the Cleaners really are attacking, the more of us who retaliate, the better.

"You take the lead, Jared," Dad whispers, joining us on the path as we reach the top of their long lane-style driveway.

Seeing a slumped figure on the floor, I charge forward holding my hand behind me and gesturing for Saskia and Dad to stay back. Crouching beside the body, I feel for a pulse. I hear a grumble of pain as I touch him, and the lion's energy pulses against my skin. He rolls onto his back, and I instantly recognise him.

"Simmo, what happened?" I ask, as I gently search his body for injuries, finding at least four bullet holes in the process.

"Jared?" He breathes my name, the pain clear in his barely-there voice. "Cleaners… ran off… gone."

At his words, I wave Dad and Saskia over. "Okay, Simmo. You rest up." I turn to Dad and Saskia. "The Cleaners ran off. They've shot him up good, and he's in a lot of pain."

Saskia crouches beside him, running a gentle hand over his head. "He's burning up." She glances from him to the pair of us with wide eyes, before her blue eyes fall back on him. "Jesus Christ, Simmo. Did they shoot you up with silver?" Simmo lets out a pained grunt in answer as he tries to curl in on himself.

Roaring, I step forward, ready to charge into the bush after the Cleaners. The fuckers need to die. A hand whips out around my bicep, holding me in place.

"Jared. Don't!" Dad orders.

Slowly and deliberately, I turn to face my father. I bite back my anger at being ordered to stay. Seeing his lion's amber eyes tells me I'm not the only one close to my beast. "The fuckers need to die." I reiterate my thoughts.

Dad releases a sharp breath. "They do." He glances down at Simmo, before looking out to the bush. "It will be pointless following them and stumbling around in the dark. If we leave it until tomorrow, we can follow them right to their base camp and wipe the lot of them out. Not just the couple that attacked here tonight."

Knowing he's right, I take a calming breath. My lion recedes, liking the thought of taking out as many Cleaners as possible. "I'm going to check in the house. See how the others are doing."

"Good," he says with a nod. "I'll call our healers and tell them to prep the medical rooms."

Striding towards the house, I pick up the scent of blood before I open the door and know someone is badly hurt. "Hello?" I call. "Pete? Rosie? It's Jared. Are you okay?"

The sound of a relieved sob comes from the back of the house, and I race towards it.

Opening a door, I step into the kitchen and am faced with Rosie crouched over Pete's body on the floor.

"*Shit!*" I say at the sight, hoping Pete's going to pull through. I don't want to deal with another female losing her mate.

"I'm not as bad as I look. I've told you, darling, most of the blood is David's." Pete lifts a hand and points around the kitchen island. "You might wanna check him out if it's safe. The bastards shot me before I got a good look at him."

"No worries mate." I round the island in a couple of long strides and lower myself over David's still body, reaching out to search for a pulse. "He's got a pulse. Thank fuck!" I tell Pete, knowing he'll be concerned. Feeling how weak it is under my fingertips, I know he won't survive if the silver stays in any longer.

My eyes roam the kitchen looking for anything I can use to dig out the bullets in David's body. Spotting a magnetised knife rack on the wall, I run my eyes along the length of it until they fall on a small paring knife. It should be the perfect size, providing it's sharp enough.

Grabbing the knife, I turn and root through the pantry looking for either medical supplies or anything I can use as a disinfectant. The silver will make his body weak and using a disinfectant will at least help guard against any infections the weakened immune system will make him susceptible to.

"What do you need, Jared?"

Lifting a bottle after bottle on the shelf, "A disinfectant," I answer, discarding an oil and picking up a white vinegar.

"That'll do it. White vinegar," Rosie states over my shoulder, sounding confident.

I frown as I weigh up the bottle. "Are you sure?"

She nods vigorously. "Lillian used to swear by it. She always used it on Benji every time he had any kind of injury. They went through gallons of the stuff."

Shrugging, I take the bottle over to David on the floor.

"Right, Davie. I'll apologise now because this ain't gonna be fun for either of us, but it needs to be done," I explain to the seemingly lifeless body before me. If it weren't for the fact that I can still feel him through the pride bonds I'd think him dead, even my supersensitive ears can't pick up his heartbeat.

Saskia's energy runs along my skin, alerting me to the fact that she's walked into the room. "Do you need help in here, Jared?" Her footsteps stop beside me, and I look up at her as I undo the bottle of vinegar and pour some over the knife.

"Pete, are you okay?" I call over my shoulder.

"Yeah, I've only got one shot in my leg, I can wait a little while longer for it to be pulled out."

I nod and rip open David's shirt, clearing the way to the wounds I know are there. "I could do with someone to hold him down if you're up for it, Sass," I answer Saskia's earlier question.

She sighs, and I think she's going to complain about my shortening her name. I'm more than surprised when she glares at me as she drops to Dave's other side. "Are you suggesting because I'm a woman I won't be able to hold him still?"

I flick my eyes to her in shock as I try to think of what the hell I said to make her think that. "What? Not at all." I shake my head, dismissing the whole conversation knowing that now is not the time for it.

"I'll take the bottom half." Not waiting for acceptance, she slides her legs over Dave's hips and effectively pins him to the floor.

Gritting my teeth in anger at the sight of her in that position with a mated man, I force myself to concentrate on the task in front of me.

Starting with the wounds in his stomach, I slice across them making them wide enough to get my fingers in and pick out the bullets. Flicking them out one by one, I release a breath before moving onto the two in his shoulder.

There's a shrill cry as the sound of footsteps on the hardwood floor get closer. "*Davie!*"

Dave groans on the floor as if the sound of his mate so close has brought him to.

"Beth." Rosie calls and I look up to see her stepping into the hysterical woman's path and pulling her to a stop. "You need to calm down. Your energy is bringing him to and he'll be able to feel everything Jared does as he gets the silver bullets out of him."

The woman—Beth—Rosie had called her, looks at me with tear filled eyes.

"I've only got two more to get out. Why don't you go for a breather outside with Rosie and I'll call you in as soon as

I'm done?" I'd made it sound like a suggestion but the alpha power I packed behind it meant it was a definite order.

"You're getting good at those alpha orders even when you aren't their alpha," Saskia mutters under her breath, knowing full well that I'd hear her.

As I slice the last two wounds Dave starts to squirm on the floor, so I pin his uninjured shoulder down with my knee before sliding my fingers into the wounds in quick succession.

Grabbing the bottle of vinegar I glance down to Dave who is no longer trying to fight me but has his unfocused eyes trained on the bottle. "This might sting," I warn before pouring the liquid liberally over all the wounds.

A pained roar leaves his mouth and I look down to see his lion's eyes looking back at me. Hearing heavy footsteps enter the house, I turn to look over my shoulder and watch my father step in. Dave instantly relaxes beneath my hands and I know Father has taken some of the pain away with his alpha power.

"Those bullets are something else. They must leave a silver residue because Simmo's wounds aren't healing even after having the bullets removed," Dad announces as he crouches beside Dave. Saskia rises off Dave's hips and moves over to beside his head, giving my father room to access Dave's wounds. He lays his hands over one of the wounds on Dave's stomach and closes his eyes.

I can feel Dad's alpha energy pulsing against my skin and watch as a bead of sweat forms on his brow. Placing my hands on top of my father's I offer him my own alpha power. I may not be alpha of this pride, but I am an alpha in my own right and power.

Dad's eyes open and lock on to mine. "Thank you." Within seconds tiny beads of silver lift to the top of the wound as if they're attracted to our energy. We fight through the stinging pain it gives us and, on Dad's cue, we lift our hands away and shake off the beads, hearing them clink as they hit each other in their fall to the floor beside us.

"Jesus, they have a bite to them. Did you do it to Simmo's wounds alone?"

Dad shakes his head. "No, I didn't think to try until I came in here."

"Are you guys going to be able to do that for all the wounds?" Saskia asks as she strokes a hand over Dave's forehead. He's out cold and probably won't even know about it, but it will help Saskia's lioness into feeling she's at least doing something.

"We'll give it a good go, Sass." I flick my eyes to Dad, belatedly realising it's his choice. "Right, Dad?"

Placing his hand over the next wound he tries to hide a small grin with the duck of his head, making it clear he picked up on my mistake. "That we will, Son."

Laying my hand over the top of his once again I push my energy through, feeling it melt into his.

6

HELPING HAND

WATCHING Grigori and Jared weakening themselves to heal the injured pride member before them, I suddenly understand what it takes to be an alpha. The strength and the sacrifice it takes. I also understand what the pride is losing with Jared having already committed to his new little pride. Thinking about the rest of our dominant pride members, I can't name one that would be willing to sacrifice his strength and power as selflessly as Grigori and Jared are right now. I just hope there's nothing that takes Grigori away from us before someone who is good enough to step up into the role of alpha joins the pride.

With my hand still on Dave's forehead I push my energy forward and feel it wrap around Grigori and Jared's energies, melding all three of us together. Neither of them reacts, probably too focused on the healing to notice what little power I'm pushing towards them. I'm not a submissive by a long shot but I'm also not an alpha. I just hope it helps them, even if it's just a little, a helping hand.

It doesn't take long to have Dave's wounds healed enough to have him out of danger. Pulling back my power, I remove my hand from contact with Dave's forehead, grateful for the fact that I wasn't in contact with the wounds and collecting those beads of silver along my skin. Jared had said they had bite and I wasn't exactly wanting to experience that.

"Is he going to be okay?" A gentle voice asks from behind Jared.

Standing, he turns to face the petite brunette. "A few days rest and he'll be fine, Beth." He gives her arm a gentle squeeze as he steps aside, giving her access to her mate.

"He's so pale," she worries, bringing her hands to her mouth in shock.

Straightening to his full six feet, Grigori pulls her into his side. "He lost a lot of blood. That's all it is." He places a gentle kiss on the top of her head. "Feel him through the bonds, he's there and his energy is steady and strengthening by the minute."

After a second or two, she takes a deep—and no doubt—calming breath, probably doing exactly as Grigori suggested. "You're right. Thank you." She flicks her eyes over her shoulder to Jared. "Both of you."

"Guy's…" Pete's wavering voice calls through the kitchen. "Not wanting to worry you but my blood is starting to feel like it's on the boil."

The three of us scattered around the kitchen bench, moving to Pete's side. I crouched beside Rosie, who has his hand in hers, knowing I need contact with him to help the guys. I discreetly placed my hand on his knee, giving a gentle squeeze. "These two will have the silver out in no time." I flick my eyes to Jared hoping I'm telling the truth. The heat coming off his skin makes me worry that the silver is actually making his blood boil.

"Dad, you ready?" Jared asks, his eyes not leaving the injured man on the floor.

Grigori places his hand over Pete's wound. "Let's do this."

Once I feel the guys' energy focusing on Pete's body, I push my energy forward with the hope that it's at least offering a little help to them.

"Oh, god…" He groans, the pain clearly getting the better of him.

Unable to see our pride mate in pain, my lioness comes to the forefront, helping me pour everything we have into Pete.

Jared's eyes connect with mine, wide and surprised, alerting me to the fact that he must be able to feel my energy now. Closing my eyes, I break eye contact, not wanting to let Jared see too much in my lioness's eyes. Having her so close to the surface makes me feel vulnerable and laid bare to him.

Within a few minutes Pete's body relaxes beneath us, a content sigh leaving his lips.

The sound is like music to my ears. As my head starts to spin, I pull my energy back and push at my lioness.

Swiping at me she pounces forward, bursting free.

Having depleted all my energy I'm unable to do anything to fight her. I can't even understand where she's getting *her* energy from.

She should be as weak as I am. The thought runs through my mind seconds before we blackout.

7

PLAYFUL PLAYBACK

SASKIA'S panicked eyes have me reaching out as her lioness hits the deck.

"Saskia?" The worry is evident by the shakiness in my voice. Running a hand over her fur, the feel of her energy has my lion relaxing.

"She's sleeping," Dad informs me, as if I hadn't already worked that one out. "She used a lot of her energy and needs to recuperate as she would if she had healed herself."

I frown. "She must have been helping with Dave too. I saw her hold onto him." I shake my head. "She could have killed herself."

A shiver runs over my skin at my words, my lion clearly distressed at the thought.

Dad clears his throat.

Realising I'm still absentmindedly stroking Saskia's fur, I pull my hand away just as a handful of pack members come in with a couple of stretchers.

A young lion called Evan glances down at Saskia. "I didn't realise any females were injured." He locks his eyes on mine questioningly.

Not feeling the need to answer his questions, I scoop her into my arms. "She's none of your concern," My lion says through my mouth, a threatening rumble obvious beneath the words.

Dad's head spins in my direction, ignoring the medic he'd just been talking with.

Before he can address me, and my actions, I stride out of the room. "I'll take her somewhere she can rest more comfortably."

It doesn't take me long to get to her little studio flat above her gran's garage. I'm not surprised to find the door wide open. If she is anything like us, she departed in a hurry, her mind on the fight ahead of her and not caring about what she left behind or how it was discarded.

Striding up the stairs two at a time, the room I step into looks just as I'd expect. One large open space divided into a kitchen, lounge and bedroom. The bedroom is at the far side, with a bed across the window, looking out onto bushland.

I place her sleeping lion on the bed and glance around the room wondering what to do now. Part of me wants to leave and another part of me is on edge at the thought of leaving.

Lions are more solitary than wolves. We don't sleep in piles—puppy piles, the wolves call them—for comfort. Touch still calms us but not in excess. Obviously it's different for mates, there's nothing more comforting than the touch of your mate and just knowing they are there, right beside you for the rest of your days.

Spotting the tree outside the window, I find the perfect solution. Its thick branches will easily hold my weight and with the window open I'll have easy access if any serious after effects happens to Saskia.

After sliding the window open I quickly pull my clothes off and shift into my lion form before settling down on a sturdy branch to sleep.

———

SOMETHING POKES at my side rousing me from sleep. Wanting just a little more sleep, I roll away and the support beneath me disappears. My eyes pop open as I drop to the ground, landing on my feet like the cat I am.

The sound of laughter draws my eyes to the window above.

"Oh…my…god!" Saskia spits out between cries of laughter. "That was almost worth waking up to find you in my tree."

Spotting the broom in her hand has me glaring at her through my lion's eyes. She poked me out of the fucking tree. I let out a roar to let her know my dissatisfaction.

Seeing her double over laughing harder makes my lion want to put her in her place and, honestly, so do I. Realising the best time to get her is while she's distracted, I pounce up the tree and through the window. I wrap my limbs around her as we fall to the floor, twisting to ensure my body takes the brunt of it before coming to a stop with her back on the floor and my paws on either side of her.

"*Jared!*" Saskia stares up at me, her head between my paws. "What the hell?"

With my lion at the forefront, I settle back, happy with him taking control of the moment. He flicks out a tongue and laps at her cheek.

She twists her head from side to side obviously trying to remove the wetness but unable to reach anything but my fur to rub it on. "For fuck's sake, Jared."

Her hands push at my underbelly trying to lift me off. "Move it you big oaf!"

We don't move an inch, just stare at her, delighted at her growing frustration. If she wanted to laugh at me when she made me fall out the tree, then she can deal with my lion's playful payback. Lowering down, my lion rubs our face on hers.

Saskia's wide eyes, have me jumping to the forefront and taking control back.

Jesus fucking Christ.

He was marking her with his scent.

Claiming her as his.

Shaking my head I step back, giving Saskia room to slip out from beneath me.

She's across the room in a nano-second. "What the fuck was that?" Her high-pitched voice tells me she's as concerned about my lion's actions as I am.

I quickly shift back into my human form, knowing the only way to take the panic away from her is to speak and I can't do that in my lion's body.

Turning to the chair I'd left my clothes on the night before I pull them on, not caring about the pain it causes against my overly sensitive skin from the shift.

"Jared, what was that? Your lion just…" She didn't finish the sentence and I was glad of it. It meant my next words would be much more believable.

"I was just trying to piss you off, and what better way to do it than to mark you with my scent?" I laugh. "It worked, right?"

She stares at me intently, obviously trying to read something on my face. I give her my best poker face as I try not to think about the fact that I have no fucking idea why my lion just did what he did. She narrows her eyes before giving me a nod. "Yeah. And now I'll have to shower a million times before I go anywhere, great!"

I smirk from ear to ear. "I'll take that as mission accomplished."

She turns with a huff and heads towards a door that must be the bathroom. "You know where the door is, since you let yourself in last night. You may as well let yourself out."

Her reminder of why I was here in the first place has me stepping up behind her and spinning her by her shoulder to face me. "What you did last night was stupid and dangerous." My voice comes out gruffer than I'd meant.

Saskia glares at me, a mask of stubborn anger covering her face. "Stupid? I only did what you did. I was trying to help a pride mate. Hell, I was trying to help my alpha and his son." She drops her eyes as the fight seems to suddenly leave her. She shakes her head. "I didn't even think it would work, let alone cause me to pass out."

Saskia's sudden change in demeanour causes my anger to slip away and my worry move front and centre. Placing a finger under her chin I gently nudge it until she lifts her eyes to mine. "I don't think it would have worked with many other lions in the pride. You're strong, but you scared me… and Dad." I quickly correct my slip of the tongue. "You scared *us*. Promise me you won't do anything like that again."

She holds my stare and shakes her head. "I can't promise that. If there's even a small chance I could do something to save someone's life, no matter how minute my effect may be…I'll do it. Every time."

I sigh, knowing there's nothing I can say to change her answer. She's a good woman who cares for her pride mates, of course she'll do everything, including risking her life, to save someone else. I suddenly feel sympathy for whomever she ends up mating because she'll keep him on his toes and have him constantly worried about what trouble she'll get herself into. For now, that concern is her alpha's and I'll have to let him know he'll need be aware of that.

Letting my hand drop back to my side, I give her a small smile. "You better jump in that shower then." I glance at my watch. "We've got to leave in ten minutes to track those fuckers from last night," I tease, wanting to lighten the mood before leaving her apartment.

"Oh, fuck, I forgot. I thought I could just hide away until at least tomorrow before I had to be within the reach of anybody's senses."

I shrug. "You don't have to come with us."

"Fuck that!" She shouts as she slams the bathroom door behind herself.

Laughing, I spin on my heel and head for the door, knowing there's no way my scent will be leaving her today, no matter how much she scrubs. Deep down a part of me is glad about that—and that thought in itself actually scares me.

8

MAYBE IT'S TIME

USING the pink mesh loofah that usually hangs on the tap, I scrub at my face knowing all I'm doing is causing my skin to get pinker and not actually lessening Jared's scent. I can't believe he'd do such a stupid thing just to piss me off. Anyone who gets within nose reach of me will be able to scent him on me and think something's going on between us. *The fucker*.

Accepting defeat, I turn off the taps and step out of the shower. It doesn't take me long to dry off and get dressed, leaving my shoulder length hair damp, knowing it will dry in the sun as we hunt.

By the time I turn from locking the front door, Jared is standing at the bottom of the drive with five other lions.

One of them catches sight of me and runs towards me, quickly sweeping me up in a hug and swinging me around. "Hey, sweet cheeks. I missed seeing your pretty face when you went on your travels."

I pat his back. "Matty, put me down. I wasn't even gone for two days."

Placing me back on my feet he frowns at me as he steps back, quickly glancing at Jared and swallowing nervously. A clear sign that he's picked up on Jared's scent.

"It's not what you think." I run a hand through my still damp hair. "*Fuck!* The guy hasn't even been back in town for twenty-four hours, do you really think…" I don't bother finishing the question, knowing if I was in Matty's shoes I'd probably be jumping to the same conclusion.

I turn my attention to Jared who is still waiting with the others at the bottom of the drive. Even from this distance I can see the flicker of gold from his lion's eyes in his face. "Jared, please…tell them."

He clears his throat. "She's right. Saskia pissed me off and that was my payback." He spins on his heels and starts striding down the road. "Come on, we've got some tracking to do."

Matty falls into step beside me as we head for Rosie and Pete's house—the starting point to pick up the Cleaners' trail.

I can't help but hope with every part of my being that Jared's nose still works as good as it once did because we've all been out of luck when tracking them after previous attacks and we really need to catch a break.

Matt clears his throat and I can hazard a guess that whatever he's planning on saying is going to be awkward. Matt is one to just blurt things out, so when he thinks before speaking you know it's a hard thing for him to say. "So, nothing happened with you two?"

"That's what we both said, didn't we? Did you sense a lie?" I ask turning my head to let him see my eyes, knowing that will speak to the truth too.

He squints, clearly trying to see something he's not, before nodding. "Okay. I won't mention it again."

We walk for a few more minutes before I can't take the tension still hanging in the air. I nudge him with my shoulder. "Can we go back to normal now?"

"Normal…Are you sure that's what you want?" Before I can even think about answering his question I'm airborne.

I let out a squeal. "Ahhh…"

After flying through the air, I'm settled over a shoulder

with a perfect view of Matt's arse—And I know it's Matt's arse because I've seen it in all its glory many times since we've been *fuck buddies* for the last couple of years.

"Matt! This isn't what I meant and you know it." As much as I try, I can't keep the laughter out of my voice.

I've always loved how playful he is, it's why our relationship works. Neither of us take it seriously. We get a scratch and the other itches it, no questions asked. And if either of us decided to sleep with someone else, or even take a mate, there'd be no hard feelings. We're fuck buddies, but first and foremost we're friends and pride mates.

An angry roar fills the air and the sound of footsteps on the hard pavement cease instantly as everyone stills. "We're splitting up!"

"Won't we be…" I start, but, feeling stupid over Matt's shoulder I pat at his back, "Put me down."

Once on my two feet I try again. "Won't we be more useful in a large group when we come across them? It'll make it an easier fight since we have no idea how many of them there are."

"We've got to find them first. We'll cover more ground this way." His eyes leave mine for a second to roam around the rest of the group before they lock back on mine. "You're with me, Saskia. The rest of you pair up, one of you needs to stay in human form at all times so we can keep in contact via our mobiles if and when we find them."

There was a round of nods, making it clear everyone agreed to his terms. I wasn't happy about being stuck with him but I didn't want to argue either, he seemed to be a snappy mood as it was. I guess he's a grumpy lion on little sleep.

"Catch you in a bit." Matt gives me a one armed hug. "Try not to get yourself into too much trouble," he adds, giving Jared a wary glance.

Tucking my loose shoulder length hair behind my ears, I let out a laugh. "We aren't paired together so I'm not with the biggest trouble maker in town." I poke my tongue out at him playfully before making my way over to Jared who's already eyeing the bushes like he can see something that interests him.

"We'll go in here. The rest of you head up the road further and drop in, in your pairs, every fifteen metres or so. Try and stay in your section, unless you pick up on a Cleaner's trail." With those words he steps into the bush and I have no option but to follow him.

As I follow behind him my mind wanders, thoughts about the Cleaners and their attacks at the forefront of my mind. If the enforcers weren't so close to Pete and Rosie's last night, the Cleaners would have killed them. They would have probably moved to the next property too. I have a feeling Grigori will be adding extra enforcers to patrols until this is all over. Let's hope we can find them today and end them once and for all.

"What are you thinking about?" Jared asks, startling me from my thoughts.

I keep my eyes on the ground to ensure hidden hazards in the ground cover don't trip me up. "The Cleaners and what could have happened last night if Simmo and Dave were at the other side of town. Why?"

"You were growling under your breath. I thought you were mad at me for splitting you and your boyfriend up."

I crash into a hard chest and look up into the golden eyes of Jared's lion. "My boyfriend? Matt?" I ask as I take a step back, knowing that's exactly who he's referring to. I don't wait for the confirmation before going on, "Matt is not my boyfriend. Never has been, never will be."

He bites his lip as he reads my face, clearly looking for something there. My finger itches to free his lip but I force my hands into my back pockets to help stop myself from reaching out and doing just that.

He runs a hand through his hair. "You're telling the truth but your scent was all over his bedroom when I had to personally wake him up this morning. Care to explain that?"

I open my mouth to do just that before biting it back down. "Not particularly. You're not my alpha, so I don't owe you any explanations." Giving him no room to argue I point ahead. "Are we going to hunt these fuckers or are you going to question my choice of underwear next?"

He lets out a grunt, making it clear he's not happy with my reply, but he doesn't push any further, turning and following whatever trail he was originally following.

After ten minutes of walking in silence he stops in his tracks and I have to stumble backwards in order not to crash into him again.

"Fuck!" I complain. "What are you stopping for?"

"Their trail stops dead." He drops to all fours and scents around the base of the shrubs.

It's such an animal thing to do, it looks funny with him in his human form and I force myself to hold back a laugh. "I told you, their scent just disappears. You'll need your lion's nose, and that's if we're lucky." I remind him, referring to our previous conversations during the trip up here.

"I know," he says as he straightens to his full height. "I just wanted to familiarise myself with the area in human form first."

I roll my eyes. "You've walked these tracks a thousand times in both forms over the years. You'd be able to do it blindfolded no matter how long you've been away." It was the truth and—going by the nod he gave me—he knew it, which made me wonder what the reason he was refusing to change to his lion form was.

After a moments hesitation he pulls his shirt over his

head, one of those 'one handed by the back of the collar' things that only men can make look like the sexiest movement ever known. I can't tear my eyes off his abs as the muscles there ripple with the movement.

Fuck!

Hanging his t-shirt over his shoulder, he deftly unhooks the button on his jeans before reaching for his zipper.

My mouth dries and I swallow. I must make some noise because Jared's eyes suddenly flick to mine as his hand freezes its movement.

The world around us seems to fade away as our eyes stay locked for what feels like the longest moment, before the sound of a zipper fills the air sounding so much louder than it really should be.

It takes everything in me to force my eyes not to drift down to what I know that zipper is uncovering. The smirk that slides across Jared's face tells me he knows how hard I'm fighting.

The sound of heavy denim hitting the floor and Jared's soft footsteps alert me to the fact that he's stepping out of them. The leaves crunch beneath his feet.

I lick my lips as sexual tension seems to crackle between us.

And I can't help but wonder what the fuck is going on. I've never been interested in Jared, so why the hell am I suddenly lusting after him now?

I haven't had sex in a while, which has left me horny. That has to be it. *Maybe it's time to get my itch scratched again.*

Jared's face starts to shift before my eyes and he drops to all fours as the rest of his body changes to his lion's. He shakes his head, the sunlight shimmering in the golden strands of his mane and I can't help but look at him in wonder. I may see lions all the time but Jared's alpha energy gives him a more majestic aura compared to the others.

Maybe that's another reason why I'm having this weird attraction to him.

Jared nudges at his clothes before eyeing me up and I let out a huff realising what he wants.

"Seriously?" I ask. When he turns and sniffs at the ground clearly getting down to business, I sigh. "Fine, but next time you can carry your own clothes." Grumbling to myself about how he should have thought to bring a backpack or something, I snatch up the offending items and fold them over my arm.

I'd leave them here if I didn't think he'd need them again if we came across a group of Cleaners. Then again, a naked Jared could maybe work in our favour as a distraction.

9

PLAYING WITH PREY

USING my lion's nose I search for any scent that shouldn't be there, forcing myself not to think about the sexual tension that had been flying between us only moments ago.

Jesus, it took everything for me to not stride up and claim her lips when Saskia had licked them.

Shaking my head to remove the thoughts, I huff out of my nose causing red dirt to blow up and into my face.

I sneeze. More dust lifts. Saskia laughs behind me and I start to turn so I can snap my teeth at her to let her know I'm not amused, only I spot something in the dirt, a patch that hasn't moved. A boot shaped patch.

I shift instantly.

"What is it?" Saskia asks, stepping up behind me.

I feel her energy brush against mine, but don't turn my attention away from the print. Instead, I rub a hand across the ground on the spot you'd expect another print to be if someone was running. Low and behold as the dust cloud settles, another boot print appears, whatever magic they've used hasn't removed the prints just covered them.

Testing a theory, I put my nose to the ground and low and behold, I picked up a scent that hadn't been there moments before.

"Is that…?" Saskia starts.

"It sure is!" I straighten and turn to face her. "Pass my

clothes and call the others, tell them they need to disturb the top layer of dirt to find any trail."

Pulling my clothes from where they'd been draped over her shoulder, she chucks them at me and I step into them as I listen to her relay the information.

Snapping a branch from a nearby tree I start sweeping in front of the boot prints, uncovering more as I go. Part of me wonders what kind of magic they've used to do something like this but another part doesn't care, we've found a way to break through the magic and that's all that matters right now.

"Jared…"

I flick my eyes to Saskia letting her know she has my attention.

She carries on, "Matty's asking, what do you want them to do if they don't find anything in their search area?"

"Come and follow our trail, we might need back up." I suggest as I turn my attention back to the tracks before me. It's clearly only one person's tracks, but the fact that we know at least two people attacked Rose and Pete means one of the other teams must have the other trail to follow.

I take a few steps back and as I weigh up the tracks I realise breaking the magic not only unearthed the foot prints in the dirt but it also made the broken twigs and branches that the person brushed against visible.

I start following the tracks, brushing the floor with the branch as I go.

The bush out here isn't always dense and after about an hours trekking we come upon a clearing.

Spotting two men sat on a couple of fallen logs beside what looks like a camping area with a tent and some other metal structure, I hold my hand out behind me in a stop gesture hoping Saskia understands my meaning as I fall into a crouch.

The sounds of her footsteps cease, and I feel her energy brush against my skin as she crouches beside me. Saskia holds up two fingers and looks at me with a raised brow.

I inhale deeply trying to pick up their scents. Scenting four different people I shake my head and hold up four fingers in answer.

Saskia nods having probably scented them for herself. Her wide eyes fall on mine making it clear she picked up the same thing as I did.

One of them isn't human. They're a shifter.

I point to myself before pointing off to the right, indicating that I'll go that way and creep up on the other side of the campsite. She nods, and I hope she waits for me to get around the other side before she starts her descent on them from this side. Unfortunately, there's no way for me to make that clear without speaking aloud, and if I do that even a whisper would be heard by the shifter.

Keeping as low to the ground as I can, I start to make my way around the edge of the clearing. Only within a couple of steps someone stomps out of the bushes—obviously not trying to be stealthy—right in front of me.

"All cl—" His sentence stops dead as he stares at me with wide eyes.

I grin as excitement flows through me at the thought of the prey within my reach. My lion is roaring inside of me wanting me to shift so we can tear him apart, but we need answers.

We know this is just a small group of them. There has to be a bigger camp out there somewhere and these guys are going to be the lucky ones to tell us where it is.

"Fuuuck!" He cries out as he makes to run towards his buddies.

I hear sounds of movement from their direction making

it obvious they've seen us and are planning on attacking or trying to leave.

Throwing my arm out I grab a hold of the guy's shirt, instantly stopping his escape. "You ain't getting away that easy," I say as I wrench one of his arms behind his back.

He cries out in pain.

Stepping in close to his back as I bend his arm at a tighter, more unnatural, angle, I have to remind myself that he's human and therefore much more breakable than the people I'm used to fighting.

I begrudgingly loosen my hold, just enough to know I'm not going to break him prematurely, as I whisper in his ear. "I've got some questions for you before I let you leave."

He gasps. "You...You're going to let me go?"

"That depends on you and what you tell me," I offer, meaning every word. He may have pulled the trigger last night or it may have been one of his buddies, but there's a bigger bad guy dishing out the orders and that's whom we need to find. If letting these dick heads go is what lets us get him, then I'll take it.

The sound of fighting catches both our attention. Our heads flick in the direction of the camp where I can see Saskia throwing punches at both the guys, a couple of metres away from where they'd been sitting. The fact that she's easily in control—neither of them managing to lay a punch on her because her reflexes are too quick for them—has me staying calm and turning my attention back to the guy in my hands.

"Wh...what do you wanna...know?" he asks. He fumbles about and I think he must be trying to ease the tension I have on his arm.

I ask the most important question. "Where's your head-quarters located?"

He stiffens and starts to stutter. "I…I…No. I can't answer that. They'd kill me."

I tug him closer towards me. "Don't tell me, and I'll kill you. I'm pretty sure I could make it more painful than they will," I threaten, ending on a growl.

Within seconds his feet shift, his legs going tense.

Having been in many fights over the years I know that's a sign of a defensive move. I wrench his hand up his back as he spins in the opposite direction; the resulting snap has me instantly letting go.

He drops to the floor, the pain having gotten the better of him and making him pass out. I stare at his limp body and make a split-second decision that he won't be going anywhere for the time being, even if he comes around the pain won't have lessened and the second he moves he'll possibly pass out again.

Sprinting across the clearing I weigh up who I need to take off Saskia's hands. I'm less than a couple of metres away when one of them draws back his hand, aiming a punch at the back of Saskia's head.

Reaching out, I spin the guy, and having already let his fist fly, I cop the hit on the mouth. I spit out a mouthful of blood before cocking back my arm and giving him a piece of his own medicine.

He throws another one my way but my reflexes are quicker than his and I manage to stay out of reach, I can tell his battle with Saskia has worn him out. His punches are getting sloppier with every fresh one he throws and, deciding we've played with our prey long enough, I end it.

In a move that I've perfected over the years, mainly in the duels I fought on Bel's behalf, I change my stance and spin on my front foot, throwing my back leg out like a baseball bat in a roundhouse kick. It hits the target, filling the air with a loud crack and my opponent crumples to the floor. It doesn't bother me that he may be dead, we have his passed out friend to tell us all about the rest of them so these two are expendable.

My lip smarts as I crouch beside the lifeless body, my fingers checking for a pulse I know won't be there, before I turn to check on Saskia. The sound of fighting has died down to nothing so I'm certain she's put the other one down too.

My eyes fall on the beautiful blonde powerhouse who gives the dead body heaped at her feet a good boot with her right foot. "Wanker!" She pulls a hand from her neck and I notice the blood it had been hiding.

I've covered the few metres that had been between us before the thought of moving even goes through my head. "Sass," I whisper as I gently turn her head to get a better view of the slice against her throat.

She bats at my hands. "It's just a nick. I'll be fine."

I can see the flow of blood has slowed as the wound has started to heal but it was no nick and, if I'm guessing right, it was made by silver because it would have stopped bleeding by now if it was an ordinary knife.

Silver is lethal to us and we know the Cleaners are aware of that, I hadn't even considered that they could have had deadly weapons before walking into the clearing. I mentally kick myself for making such a stupid mistake. We're lucky they hadn't thought to use the guns they'd used at Rosie and Pete's.

My lion urges me to lick at her wound to clean away the toxins left from the silver. I have to force myself to not follow through with the action. She isn't my mate.

Yet. The word flows through my head.

Never. I send back to the lion within.

"The fact that you let him get that close to you with silver has me worried. I knew I should have gone after them alone." My anger turns from her to myself for even allowing her to be near the danger. Why had I even brought her on the hunt today? I could have sent her to one of the sections I knew they wouldn't have taken.

Images of her fighting, holding her own with the two guys attacking her, flow through my head and I know I'm being stupid. She's strong and can handle a fight, treating her any differently would be disrespectful and I've never been like that.

"It looks like someone got a good hit in with you too. And if my eyes aren't deceiving me, he had silver knuckle dusters on." She jabs a finger at my already smarting lip causing it to sting more.

I'd not really paid attention to what the guy had on his knuckles when he clobbered me one but, flicking my tongue out and feeling the crack still fresh in my lip, it makes sense that silver had been involved otherwise it would be healed by now.

Movement catches my eye and I look up to find Saskia leaning into me. Her eyes glued to my lips. I freeze on the spot, not wanting to break the spell between us. She licks at her own lips, so close I can feel her breath clinging to the wetness on mine.

Her soft lips press against mine and I close my eyes ready to lose myself in her taste. Our lions' energies crackle as they flow together over our skin, sending a shiver down my spine.

The sound of leaves rustling and raised voices have my eyes popping open and Saskia jumping away from me. She crouches down making a show of feeling for the dead guy's pulse. "He's dead," she announces loudly so the others can hear her, standing to her full height.

"No shit," I whisper, grinning as I watch her look anywhere but at me. "Took you long enough to get here. It's a good job we didn't need back up," I call out to the others as I count six of our guys coming out of the bush.

Matt comes charging over the clearing, skidding to a stop in front of Saskia. "Sass, fuck." He reaches out to touch her, obviously shaken by the amount of blood on her clothes, but before he can make contact Saskia steps back out of his reach.

"I'm fine, Matt." She swings her eyes over the clearing before turning them on me. "Where's the third guy?"

My eyes widen in surprise. The third guy had completely slipped my mind. Without a word I jog over the clearing coming to a stop where I'd left him, glancing down at nothing but dirt and dried out grass. Feeling her stop beside me I answer her question. "The fucker's gone, must have scrambled away while we were distracted…with the other guys." I point to the tree line and were there's an easily noticeable broken branch. He was in too much pain to worry about leaving a trail.

"He'll be easy enough to catch up with," Matt says from beside us as he strides towards the trail.

Throwing my arm out I grab his shirt, halting his steps. "Wait. Let him go."

Seven sets of eyes frown at me as though I've lost my mind.

"He's in pain and injured, he's going to be heading straight to the rest of his people," I explain. "We're going to let him lead us right to them."

Matt steps forward. "Let me go."

My eyes roam the rest of the group before me as I try to make a decision about who would be best to send. It doesn't take me long to realise it's me that needs to it. This is, after all, what my father called me back for.

I shake my head. "I'm going. The rest of you should strip this place; get whatever information you can from it and then head back to the pride. Be careful though, we scented a shifter when we arrived, but they never showed their face—not even to help fight." I focus my attention on Matt. "My father will want an update. Let him know I won't engage. It's just recon." The fourth person hadn't slipped my mind, but when they didn't jump in the fight, it made me think they may have already left the area before we arrived or they could have been an earlier kill for the Cleaners, their scent just lingering in the air.

He nods. "Consider it done."

Following my orders without question the guys head towards the campsite.

Matt pauses after only a couple of strides. "Sass, are you coming?"

Saskia stands before me biting at her lip. "No, I'm going with Jared. He might need the backup if he comes across another campsite."

I don't argue. I hadn't given her the order to go back because part of me wanted her with me. A part of me that also didn't want her with all those males, especially one that clearly had feelings for her. But I didn't want to own up to that and I know if I opened my mouth those words may come out.

I nodded, making it clear I was happy with her decision before making my way to the trail that will lead us to our enemy. Excitement flows through me from my lion at the prospect of getting to hunt down our prey once again.

10

IN CHAINS

JARED

IT'S dark by the time we come across another campsite. Scenting the air like we had last time, I pick up the scent of three humans and one shifter, just like last time. My eyes connect with Saskia's; my hands itch to rub away the frown between her eyes so I shake them out at my sides to rid them of the urge.

"He's here," I mouth. The injured guy is one of the three humans I can scent. She nods and trains her eyes on the lone guy sat by a campfire.

My ears perk up at the sound of an animal's whimper. There's a clang of metal and a man shouts out, "Stop your fucking whining, no-one is going to rescue you!"

My lion wants to charge forward but I hold him back. We can't help if we go charging in, we need to wait and assess the dangers that could be lurking in the shadows. My alpha energy pulses and the animal silences instantly.

I run a hand through my hair as we watch and wait.

Saskia shifts from foot to foot and I know it's all she can do to stop herself from moving forward.

We manage five minutes before I can lie in wait no longer. With one last glance at Saskia, I nod, giving her the go-ahead as I start for the guy by the fire shifting my fingers into claws on the way.

My hand goes around the guy's neck, my claws digging

in before he even knows what has happened. "Where are the other two?" I ask getting straight to the point.

He makes a choking noise and I loosen my hold realising I may have been squeezing too tight for him to actually talk.

"Gone…Only me." He coughs. "Here."

"Gone where?" I let my nails slice into his skin a little more as I wait for his reply.

"The warehouse. About ten k's away." He sniffles and I smell the unmistakable scent of urine. "Please don't kill me. I'll tell you anything."

The scent of his fear in the air has my lion coming to the surface. He wants to come out and play, but we don't have time for that, so I push him back down promising he'll get another chance soon.

We need to get to this warehouse and gather whatever information we can before heading back to the pride and updating my father. We'll have to make a plan of attack quickly, before they decide to move on or call in more troops.

"Jared, you need to see this," Saskia's voice calls out from behind the Cleaner's tent. Her anxious tone has me making quick work of snapping the guy's neck and moving at double speed to get to her.

"What's wrong?" I clear the campfire and instantly have the answer to my own question.

There's a scraggly looking Tasmanian Tiger cub chained to a post that's been speared into the ground. Its scent has the distinct feminine tone to it. Its pain and fear is over-powering.

Ignoring the fact that I'm facing an animal that is meant to be extinct, I drop my voice and slow my momentum as I approach her. "Hey there, little tiger."

At the sound of my voice the cub scuttles back until the chain pulls at its neck, causing blood to well around it and making me realise that the collar connected to the chain must be somehow imbedded in the flesh.

Fuckers!

Anger surges through me, but I push it down not wanting to give the cub a reason to be scared of me. "We're not here to hurt you. We came to stop those men that had you." I point over my shoulder in the direction of the body as I glance around looking for something I could use as a bandage. Not seeing anything I pull off my shirt and start to rip it up.

"If you let me come closer I might be able to remove the chain. My friend Saskia is going to go get some water." I keep my eyes on the cub and hope Saskia does as I suggest. Hearing her footsteps disappear into the tent tells me she is doing exactly that.

The Tasmanian Tiger cub cowers as I take some tentative steps towards it but it doesn't move away.

Taking that as invitation I move closer, dropping to my knees before it and placing the strips of shirt on the floor beside me.

Seeing the cub shaking like a leaf I know I need to comfort it before attempting to remove the chain.

Gently cradling its face between my hands and channelling the alpha in me I release my energy, hoping it offers some form of security and comfort.

The shaking stops and I stroke my hands through the fur, over the head and down to the chain. "That's it little cub. I'll try not to hurt you but I need to get this chain off."

The cub whimpers but doesn't move away so, taking that as encouragement, I feel around the chain and try to find how it's imbedded in the skin. The burning on my fingers as my flesh comes in contact with the cool metal tells me it's silver.

Aware of the pain this child must be going through, I

ignore my own discomfort and pick up the pace in my ministrations hoping to remove the chain as quickly as possible.

Finding a cut in the flesh of the cub's neck, I place my
head as close as possible. I hold it steady with one hand as I
push my finger against the cut, allowing my finger to feel its
way along a two centimetre spike imbedded into the skin.

Looking around the collar made from the chain, I
discover seven similar spikes spaced out evenly along it. I
almost punch the air in excitement when I come across a link
that is connected to another with a carabiner clip.

"Okay, so I have good news and bad news." I stroke my
hands down over the cub's back hoping to give it some
comfort from my touch. "I can remove it, but it's going to
hurt. A lot."

The cub's back stiffens and she jerks her head in a short
sharp nod.

I start to peel the chain off the cub's neck before she can
change her mind.

She flinches as the first spike parts with her skin.

"Sweetheart, I know this hurts but you need to stay still. I
don't want the spikes in the chain to cause anymore damage
than they already have." I glance around to find Saskia
standing behind me, being careful not to block my light from
the blazing fire. With the sun starting to set it was something
I desperately needed. "Sass, could you hold her steady?"

Saskia nods and I turn my attention back to the cub. "Is
that okay with you, Little Tiger?"

She huffs out a breath that more than likely has nothing
to do with Saskia or any pain she may be feeling, and everything to do with my calling her Little Tiger. Especially if the
glare she's giving me has anything to do with it.

Saskia does exactly as I asked and holds her steady as I
ease out each spike with the removal of the chain. Throwing
the chain aside, I wish I could bring the guy I killed earlier

back to life just so I could torture him in the same way he had tortured this cub.

Knowing there are more of them out there that we need to find and stop lets me swallow down my anger and focus on the cub. Saskia releases her and she drops to the floor, clearly unable to hold herself up any longer.

"Did you manage to find any water, Sassy?" I ask, not taking my eyes off the injured cub. She could do with some meat to help her heal.

A one-litre bottle appears before me and I take it from Saskia's hand before gently pouring it over the cub's neck, hoping to rinse away some of the toxins left over from the silver.

Moving gently so not to cause any unnecessary pain, I wrap my makeshift bandages around her neck in a scarf like fashion. "Okay." I stroke my hand over her back offering up as much comfort as I could. "You rest up. Saskia and I will be just over there having a little chat about what to do now."

Saskia walks off in the direction I'd just pointed and I follow once the little cub relaxes under my hand, almost sinking into the ground.

"We need to call the others in for clean up," Saskia offers.

"No!" I snap unable to hold back my anger at her suggestion. "No-one is coming anywhere near the cub. We'll take her to my parents, then we'll bring the others out for clean up."

She flinches at my anger, causing me to rein it in. "What the hell? She's a cub, the pride won't hurt her."

I let out an angry laugh. "What, like they didn't hurt Rosabel?" She knows as well as I do that Bel was hurt well before she was an adult—all because she was a wolf. There are plenty of ways to hurt someone without being physical.

"She isn't Rosabel. She's a Tasmanian Tiger. I'm sure Melvin and Martha would want to take her in until we can find her family, or for as long as is needed." She glares at me like I'm the one suggesting something evil.

I glare back and lower my voice. "Tasmanian Tigers are supposed to be extinct, they aren't feline like we are, even if there are similarities. Lily and Jack wanted to take Bel in—that wasn't the issue; it was the rest of the pride. They won't welcome her with open arms because she isn't one of us. She's a marsupial. They'll feel threatened eventually, just like they were with the wolf pup."

Saskia thrusts her hands in her pockets and walks away into the bush, clearly considering what I'd said.

I take the moment to check on the cub, walking over and crouching down before her. Her nose crinkles and her tongue pokes out to taste my scent but her eyes don't open. "How are you doing?" I ask as I pull one of the strips of shirt back to look at the wounds on her neck. The bleeding looks to have eased but the wounds haven't closed at all. Considering the silver toxins, her obvious malnutrition, and an estimation of her age, it will probably take a few days for her to fully heal.

The physical wounds anyway.

"Do you think you could walk for a little while? I think we should get moving, I'd like to take you to my parents' home." She lets out a whimper and I quickly carry on. "Just until we can find your family."

She shakes her head vigorously.

"You don't want to go to my parents'?" I watch, waiting for her to acknowledge my question, but her stillness makes me realise she was disagreeing with something else I'd said. "You don't have a family?"

A lone tear runs from her eye and I stroke my hand over her head and down her snout, wiping it away.

Leaves crinkle behind me as Saskia's energy comes closer, catching the cub's attention and she gets to her feet.

"As much as I hate to admit it, you're right. The pride will never fully accept another species into it." My eyes widen in surprise at Saskia's change of heart, standing up I watch as the cub takes a few tentative steps. "You need to take her back to Mount Roxby with you," she suggests. Something I'd already planned on doing the minute she'd made it clear she had no family. Saskia watches the cub for a few seconds before turning her gaze on me. "She can't make the trek back, we should call the others in. They can bring us a car and clean up this place."

I sigh. I know she's right. The protector in me wants to take the cub to Mount Roxby right now, but I can't leave Quilpie. Not while the pride still needs me. I need to stick around and help my dad bring down these Cleaners once and for all.

"Okay," I nod. "Call Matt, tell him to bring someone with him. We'll drop the cub off to my parents, they'll keep her safe, and then I'll go check out the warehouse."

Without a word Saskia pulls out her phone and calls Matt, walking away a few steps before he answers. Her walking away doesn't give her any privacy since I can hear every word she says, but it does mean I can't hear Matt's replies over the crackling fire.

Not wanting to leave a fire in the middle of our lands—bush fires are dangerous and easily get out of hand in the dry grasses and the desert heat of the Northern Territory—I call out to Saskia, "Sass, tell Matt to bring some water to put this fire out, I don't want to leave it burning overnight."

Crouching down beside the cub—who had dropped her body back into the dirt, obviously having heard our plans—I run my hand over her head. "How are you holding up, Little Tiger?"

She lets out a grumbling noise, probably at my pet name, but doesn't move.

I scratch just behind her ear, knowing it's a place that feels good when I'm in animal form. "I guess you heard the plan. Someone will be here with a car soon, so we can get you somewhere warm and safe."

She lifts her head just enough to nudge my other hand with her snout; a move that comforts *me* more than she could know.

I hate to think what horrors she's been through at the Cleaners' hands, but to see the trust she has in me already gives me hope. Hope that she hasn't been damaged too much to be the carefree girl she should be.

11

DISTRACTED

I CAN'T TEAR my eyes off of Jared as I slide the phone back in my pocket. Watching him with the cub has my lioness's interest piqued. Why? I don't know.

He's an alpha, of course he's going to be caring.

What the hell?

I shake my head, deciding I'll probably never understand where her head's at. "He said he'll be here in ten," I call out, letting Jared know what's happening in case he couldn't hear the conversation fully.

In the light of the fire I see his tongue poke out to wet his lips—lips I know are soft and gentle—and my mind instantly goes to the moment we had earlier. That fraction of a second kiss before the guys turned up.

Neither of us had mentioned the kiss once we were alone afterwards, and the walk to this camp was a long one. I don't know if we were both too focused on the trail we were following, or just avoiding discussing it completely. Mine was the latter for sure. Hell, this is the first time I've even let myself think about it.

"Sass…Are you alright?" Jared asks.

My eyes snap to his. The sight of his furrowed brow confuses me and I feel a crease forming between my own.

"I was asking you who Matt was bringing with him. You were totally spaced out."

My eyes widen in surprise. It's hard to believe I could have been so distracted that I hadn't even noticed him talking to me. "Sorry." I once again shake my head trying to focus on what he'd just asked…Matt. "Matt didn't mention it. I can call back and ask if it's important."

Jared waves it off. "No, it's all good."

Practically ten minutes to the second, Matt comes ambling through the bush. "Jesus. I never thought we'd get to you. Do you know how hard it is following that blinking dot? For future reference, maps don't show any of the obstacles that are hidden in the dark bushland." He rubs at his knee before taking in the campsite. His eyes fix on the cub laid by Jared's feet. "Holy shit, is that…? No freaking way!"

A threatening growl comes out of Jared's throat as he turns to face Matt, and Will, who just stepped out of the bush behind Matt. "Yes, it is. And you're going to pretend you haven't seen her. No one except whoever is here tonight will know about her. Understood?"

Matt and Will both nod, eyes dropped to the floor in submission.

A problem with what Jared said pops in my head and I can't help but ask him about it, "Jared, if you're planning on taking her back to town, they'll catch her scent as soon as anyone gets near."

"Yes, but they won't know what she is unless they lay eyes on her. And they won't do that unless my father deems it okay," Jared explains.

Anger boils within me and I can't hold my tongue. "You don't trust the pride at all. Have you been away for so long that you've forgotten you're one of us?"

There's an audible gasp and I know it's come from Matt and Will. Even part of me can't believe my own outburst.

Jared shakes his head, sadness in his eyes. "No, Sass… I

just remember how discriminating the pride can be towards other species."

I roll my eyes. Rosabel again. The wolf. "If I remember rightly anyone who really had something against Rosabel challenged her to a duel, and most of the hard-core haters didn't make it out of those duels alive." I sigh. "Like I said earlier, no one will harm her. Especially not while you are looking out for her." I drop my head as I lower my eyes in submission, knowing I've spoken out of turn. He's my alpha's son. Hell, he's next in line to *be* my alpha. I should never have spoken to him like that.

A finger comes into my line of sight, reaching under my chin and lifting it.

I raise my gaze to find the golden eyes of Jared's lion staring back at me.

"Don't submit. You've said nothing that I didn't need to hear. I deserved your anger." At my nod of acknowledgement, he drops his finger and I suddenly miss the feel of his lion's energy along the edge of my jaw.

Jared holds my stare for a few seconds longer than he needs to before turning his attention to Matt and Will. "I shouldn't expect you to keep secrets from the pride. Not one as important as another predator in their territory. I apologise for that."

The guys both nod in acceptance but I can see Matt's mouth is in a tight line, which suggests he wants to say something and is trying his hardest not to.

"Go ahead, get it off your chest, Matt," Jared says, making it clear I'm not the only one that can read Matt.

Matt sighs. "For what it's worth, I think you are right to be wary." My eyes narrow on Matt and I realise he was biting his tongue for my sake, not Jared's. "Sorry Sass, but you don't get to see the shitty side of the arseholes in the pride. They're too busy trying to seduce you to be themselves around you."

I shake my head, unable to believe what he's saying. I'm good at reading people. Surely, if there were a number of arseholes, like Matt is suggesting, I'd be able to see through their shit; at least with most of them anyway.

Jared nods. "I appreciate that, Matt. How far is the vehicle? I'm not sure she'll make much of a distance on her own," he states, referring to the cub.

He's right in what he said. She looks beat and now that she feels somewhat safe with Jared and his lion's company, her adrenaline seems to be zapped. It's not like one of us could carry her either. No matter how much she trusts Jared, he's still essentially a stranger. Her animal won't allow him to be that close so soon. Depending on what they may have done to her, or what she may have seen in the Cleaners' care, she may never let anyone that close to her for a very long time.

"It's only five hundred metres to the west. They must have chosen this clearing because it was close to the road. Being human they maybe didn't want to travel so far by foot."

"Are you guys okay to deal with the clean up? I'll come back once I've got the cub settled in pride territory," Jared asks.

I head towards the tent, planning to help Matt and Will with the clean-up.

"Sassy, can you come with me? Just in case we hit any problems on the road. We don't know if they've sent anyone back to be with him," Jared says, hooking a thumb over towards the dead guy.

He's right. I'd completely forgotten that there could be more Cleaners coming back to the camp. I find myself suddenly wondering if Matt and Will will be safe if a group of cleaners arrive after we left. Before I can voice my concerns, Matt speaks up.

"Actually, Grigori is waiting in the truck, so you'll have plenty of lion power between the two of you if Saskia wanted to stay and help us out here."

My eyes flick to Jared as curiosity runs through me over how he'll react to Matt's suggestion. He's been very insistent on me being paired up with him today.

Jared's eyes lock onto Matt's, narrowing, as Matt stared back. When Matt nodded it seemed as though they'd been having a conversation with just the look and it left me wondering if Jared already has the ability to talk to pride members without being in animal form like his father can, even though he isn't our alpha. I'll be sure to ask Matt that once we get a minute of privacy.

Jared spun on his heel and crouched beside the Tasmanian Tiger cub. "Okay. Little Tiger, are you ready to go?" His hand gently brushed over her head and she cracked one eye, the firelight glistening in it as she stared at him.

I laughed, realising she wasn't impressed with the name he'd called her.

"When you shift and tell me your name, I'll stop calling you that but until then…it's Little Tiger," Jared says, clearly catching onto the same thought as me.

She huffs and gets up, turning and heading west, making it obvious that she'd been listening to our conversation all along and not actually sleeping like I'd assumed.

I stare after them as they walk through the bushes, watching much longer than the time it took for them to disappear. Someone clears their throat, pulling me out of my daze, and I train my eyes on Matt, who's looking at me his eyes brimming with concern.

A quick dart of the eyes to Will and I can see he's got curiosity written all over his face.

"What's that look for?" I ask, unable to take the silence hanging in the air as I look from one to the other, not caring who answers.

"There's something going on between you two," Will announces with a shrug.

I scoff. "Me and Jared? You are so wrong."

"When you two are in the same vicinity the sexual tension is palpable. If you're in denial about it, your lioness isn't," Will adds and I look to Matt to see if he agrees.

The smile on Matt's face is a sad one, which tells me it all, but I still ask, "You think so too?"

He nods. "Sorry, Sassy, but I agree, which means we can no longer be fuck buddies."

My jaw drops at his words. "What the fuck? Are you serious?"

Matt lifts his arms in surrender. "I am, Sass. I'd like to see my next birthday," he admits, not a hint of humour in his voice.

I sigh, but stiffen my back—not wanting to seem as hurt and rejected as I feel—before turning my attention to Will. "Fine… What about you, Will? Fancy a roll in the hay, once again?"

Will and I had dated for about a year, well before Matt and I made our fuck buddies deal. In the end we'd split because he wanted to dip his dick elsewhere. Just the reminder made me wish I hadn't made him the offer.

"No chance. I wanna live a little longer too." Will shakes his head vigorously.

Unable to look at the pair of wusses any longer, I stride towards the tent without another word, ducking inside as soon as I reach it.

I can't believe they think something is going on between Jared and me. Yes, there is some sexual tension but we're sexual animals, of course there's going to be tension. Hell, if

I was left in close vicinity with any attractive single male for the length of time I had been with Jared today, there would be sexual tension.

I shake my head, as I try to dispel the thoughts of sex—after all, it doesn't look like I'll be getting any in the near future—and focus on the items lying around in the tent.

12

SAFE PLACE

JARED

"JUMP IN, LIL' Tiger," I say, waving an arm into the dual cab truck as I hold the door open. She lets out a little growl, no doubt in protest to the nickname, which makes me smile.

Although I offered to call her by her real name—if only I knew it—I don't think I'll be able to call her anything but Little Tiger even after she tells me her name.

She lays out, stretching across the whole seat, making it clear to me she wants it all to herself. I'd thought she'd maybe want me close since she doesn't know the other predator in the car, but perhaps she's happy being the one with the advantage since we'll have our backs to her and she could attack us at any moment. Or at least that's what her tiger will be thinking.

Dad stays silent while I slip into the passenger seat, probably not wanting to spook the cub.

"Hey, Dad," I greet him, wanting Little Tiger to know he's a safe person.

He starts the engine and pulls away, spinning the car around on the deserted road back to pride territory. "So, fill me in, it's been a long day."

I frown, glancing across at him. "Didn't Matt tell you everything?"

"He did, but I want to hear it from you. I want your take on it." Dad keeps his eyes on the road while I think about what to say.

"We need to destroy them." I take a quick look over my shoulder, checking on Little Tiger, who seems to be asleep but I know she won't be. Her tiger won't let her, not until she feels completely safe and that will probably only be when she's alone.

"We do," Dad agreed.

I run a hand through my hair and swallow hard, suddenly realising I'm both hungry and thirsty. We've been out since dawn, only eating a protein bar or two that we'd found at the first camp while we were searching for the second; it wasn't enough for such a long trek.

"There are some steak sandwiches and a couple of bottles in the bag by your feet." A small smile spreads across Dad's lips. "Your mum didn't want you to starve."

Grabbing the bag I lift it onto my knee as I root through it. "I bet she fed everyone else that went out today, too."

He laughs. "You know her too well. She's still feeding them now."

A snout nudges against my ear and I laugh. "Hang on Lil' Tiger, it's coming." Making quick work of pulling one of the sandwiches apart, I barely have a juicy steak held up to my shoulder before it's ripped from my fingertips and Little Tiger is disappearing into the back of the cab again with her food.

"Jesus, did they not feed you?" I shake my head. "Of course they didn't," I mutter as I realise that they'd never planned on letting her live so why would they bother feeding her. She was just their trophy. Being a Tasmanian Tiger, she would have been a priceless trophy too. Dead or alive.

Dad releases a low growl. "They need stopping."

I nod. "We know their main base is in a warehouse not far from the camp site. As soon as we have Little Tiger settled in, I'll head back to the others and we'll check it out."

Dad doesn't agree instantly like I expect. Instead, he

stares ahead as we pull into the main street of town. He doesn't speak until he pulls up on his drive. "You do not engage at all, it's just recon. I don't want your emotions getting the better of you. We need to know what we are facing and make a plan so we can wipe them out."

Agitation runs through me at the thought that he doesn't trust me to keep my head in the game. "You really think I'd run in there, all guns blazing and risk our chance at destroying them?" I feel my brow furrow tightly.

He turns his body slightly in his seat as he faces me. "No, Son. I'm just making sure you're aware of the fact that your emotions may try talking a little louder once you're there."

My body relaxes with his words and I take a calming breath before nodding my acceptance of his explanation.

Dad exits the car and I follow suit.

"Bring the bag in with you, Jared. And don't forget your cub, too," Dad calls over his shoulder.

As I reach for the bag out of the foot well, Little Tiger jumps onto the passenger seat from the back and I laugh at her eagerness. "I guess that steak did you good." I lean back with the bag in my hand and she jumps out of the car. I shake my head and let out a brief laugh as she waits at my heels for me to close the door.

Mum is standing behind the kitchen island when we walk in, and half a dozen pride members are sitting at the table eating their way through some really juicy steaks.

"Jared!" Mum rounds the counter, her pink floral apron tied around her waist, and pulls me into a hug.

I chuckle. "I haven't been gone that long."

She leans back, holding me at arms' length. "You've been in Mount Roxby for a long time. I'm going to make the most of the hugs while you're home."

Grinning, I press a kiss to her cheek before stepping back

and gesturing towards Little Tiger, who'd managed to hide herself behind me. "Mum, this is Lil' Tiger."

When she huffs once again at the mention of the name I crouch down with a laugh.

Cupping her snout I look into her eyes. "Until you shift and tell me your name, that's what I'm calling you, so you'll just have to get used to it."

"Holy shit, is that a what I think it is?" Someone calls out behind me. Little Tiger starts to shake, making me instantly regret bringing her through here knowing people would still be here.

"This is a safe place, remember?" Her black eyes bore into mine and I know she's trying to read how much she can trust me as we both ignore the whispers behind us. "No one will hurt you here, I promise."

Mum crouches down beside us, her knees cracking as she does, the noise causing Little Tiger to flick her eyes to my mother. "Hi, there." She holds out her hand allowing Little Tiger to scent her, and I release my hold on her snout so she can. "I bet you're hungry. Shall we find you something to eat?" It was a question, but Mum doesn't give her a chance to react. Instead she takes her time getting to her feet and steps back around the counter.

Grabbing a steak off the chopping board, Mum places the raw meat on a plate before coming back around the counter and placing it at Little Tiger's feet.

Little Tiger looks at me for permission and after I give her a slight nod she dives in.

I focus my attention back to Mum whom watches Little Tiger for a moment before turning back to the hot plate and the steaks she was searing. Within seconds she's plating one up and sliding it across to me.

"Thanks Mum." I cut in to the steak as the feel of fur brushing against my calf distracts me. Glancing down, I watch Little Tiger settle once again at my feet and hope that her clinginess doesn't last too long.

Mum sears the last steak and slides it across to my dad who just stepped into the room. After a quick glance from the steak to the empty bench top he turns his attention to Mum. "I bet you didn't feed yourself did you?"

She gives him a guilty look before turning towards the fridge. "I'll find something else for me."

Grabbing a knife and fork he cuts the meat on his plate into bite sized chunks. "No, you'll come and sit beside your mate and let him feed you."

Seeing the love in her eyes as she watches him over her shoulder fills my heart with hope. Hope that one day I'll find a love like that. Having been surrounded by mated people in Mount Roxby has made me feel lonely. Having Alyssa and Lee to look after has helped push that down but that doesn't fill the gap of a mate. If anything, seeing her pain over the loss of hers makes me wish for it more. I don't want to go through life without ever experiencing that love. A love that could leave you in pieces if you lost it.

13

MISSION OR TRAP

A FAMILIAR SCENT washes over me, piquing my lioness's attention. I snap my head to the bushes on my right and my eyes fall on Jared as he steps into the light of the opening.

"Hey," he states, his eyes instantly locking onto mine. "How's the clean-up going?"

I shrug. "There wasn't really a lot to do. There was nothing of interest left. A bag with some food rations and such, just like the last campsite."

"Oh…" Jared slips off a backpack I hadn't noticed and pulls out a foil wrapped parcel before offering it to me. "This is for you."

I take it with a frown on my face but once I bring it closer I don't need to wonder what it is, as the scent of steak wafts from the split on the foil and my stomach growls at the delicious smell. "Oh, I could totally kiss you right now."

Realising what I'd said I glance at Jared and find him stock-still. An intense gaze I'm unable to read is on his face.

"Figuratively speaking, of course," I quickly add, hoping to defuse the crackling of energy between us.

A throat clears behind me. "Jared. We're pretty much finished here, are we heading to the warehouse on foot or taking the ute?" Matt asks.

The tension leaves my body and, after another growl from my stomach, I remember the steak in my hand.

Turning from the guys I walk over to the logs by the fire and sit down as I tuck into my steak sandwich. It's cooked to perfection and I make a mental note to thank Mrs Dorfman when we get back to pride territory.

As I swallow down the last mouthful a bottle of water appears over my shoulder and I glance up at Jared, giving him a grateful smile. "Thanks."

"We're ready to go as soon as you are. Is your stomach satisfied enough to not give us away with its almighty growls or do we need to go back for more?"

Twisting the lid off the bottle I screw up my face as if I'm really contemplating my answer. "I think we'll be safe," I say before taking a good swig of the water.

"Are you gonna drink the rest of that?" Matt asks and I look up to find him gesturing to what's left of my water.

Deciding I was done, I pass the bottle over, feeling somewhat grateful for not having to carry the bottle around with me for the rest of the trip. I stand and focus on Jared, who seems to be giving Matt a death stare. "Alright, Boss Man. I'm ready."

Jared gives his head a shake as if he's dismissing something before acknowledging me. "Okay. I've left the ute by the road but I think it's best for us to go on foot. It'll be easier to be stealthier that way. Remember, we don't know what kind of safety measures they have set up, so watch your step." He pins me with a demanding stare. "They'll know our territory is close by and probably have traps set accordingly."

"Hell, the whole warehouse could be one big trap for all we know," I announce unable to keep my concerns to myself.

Jared nods. "That may be the case but we need to stop these Cleaners if we can. They can't be allowed to go on like they are."

My lioness straightens at Jared's determined tone. She wants to do all she can to ensure his wishes are fulfilled. I watch him walk through the campsite towards the edge of the dense bushland and silently wonder why she's reacting to him like this as I follow along behind. She's never been overly interested in any of the males in the pride, and that's including Jared when he used to live with us.

We walk for twenty minutes before Jared's pace slows. I channel my lioness's senses as I take in our surroundings, trying to pinpoint what he must have picked up on, finding a number scent trails, which makes me think this is a high traffic area.

"I think we've found their patrol track. There are too many scents for it to be anything else," Jared states as though reading my thoughts. After receiving a quick nod of agreement from us all, he starts to follow the trail and we follow him.

The scents are so strong I almost laugh at the fact they are unknowingly leading us directly to them. I pause midstep, grabbing the back of Jared's shirt so he doesn't take another step.

Matt and Will come to a halt behind me, a little too late as Matt barrels into me.

"Fuck! What did you stop for?" Matt mutters, he sounds pissed but I know it's most probably because the fact that he crashed into me shows he wasn't paying any attention when he should have been. He's more than likely pissed at himself for being side tracked and getting caught out.

"The scents are too strong," I explain. "Even if they walked this route on a daily basis—all ten people I can pick out—they wouldn't be all on top of each other like they are. Some would be more faded, others would be in different spots, even if it was only by half a metre."

Jared slowly spins on the spot, taking in our surroundings. I catch a glimpse of his lion's golden eyes as he faces me and my own lioness pushes to the forefront, wanting to be ready if she's needed.

"You're right." There's a growl behind his words and I don't understand what it means but, considering we're in the middle of what is looking more and more like a trap, now is definitely not the time to try and analyse that.

I play with the ring on my finger, suddenly regretting not taking it off before leaving home. If I shift with it on I'm likely to lose it and if I put it in my shorts pocket, it's likely to go missing when I'm getting dressed or in transportation if someone has to carry my clothes.

"Here." Jared holds out his hand towards me. "I'll put it in the backpack," he states hooking a finger over his shoulder as he gestures towards the item I'd forgotten he even had. "That way if you have to shift you won't lose it."

I frown. "What if you shift? The bag is more than likely to break if you shift with it on your back."

Jared shakes his head. "I'm not shifting. One of us needs to stay in human form and that's gonna be me. If shit hits the fan, I'll be the sacrifice. You three will return to pride territory and tell Dad to call in any help he can to protect our home."

Matt and Will both nod their agreement like the good little lions they are, but I can't. I can't agree to just leave him in the Cleaners' hands. Not after seeing what they've done to other shifters.

"Not a chance in hell!"

A low growl fills the air and I know I've got one pissed off lion on my hands before I even feel Jared's anger licking at my skin.

"Don't you dare use your alpha powers against me. You are not my alpha."

His lion's golden eyes bore into mine as he lets out a deep breath. I'm vaguely aware of Will and Matt behind me and I don't miss their gasps of surprise at my words. I don't let it distract me, there's nothing that will cause me to break eye contact with Jared. I want him to know I'm not submitting to him. Not in regards to this anyway.

Even if I wanted to obey his wishes, my lioness won't allow it.

14

DEFIANCE

JARED

TAKING A SECOND DEEP BREATH, quickly followed by a third doesn't help calm me at all. I fist my hands at my sides, feeling my nails bite into the flesh of my palms. She may be right in the fact that I'm not her alpha but I've been put in charge of this mission *by* her alpha and she should respect that. Regardless of that, it's her own order to not use my alpha powers on her that is rubbing my lion up the wrong way.

The man in me though, he's finding her defiance pretty damn sexy.

"Saskia Jayne Beaumont, I've been put in charge of this mission by your alpha and if you respect him at all, you'll follow my orders."

She stares me down and gives a slow nod of her head. I can tell by the grimace on her face it's reluctant, and the flickering of her eyes from human to animal makes it perfectly clear her lioness is fighting her.

Once her eyes stay the brown of her lioness's, I know which side of her won the fight. What I don't know is which thought each of them was backing.

"You have a pride waiting for you back home. Being the sacrificial lamb will leave them alpha-less and I will not play a part in that." Her words are final.

I open my mouth to argue but listening to her reasoning I don't have a valid argument. She's right in the fact that I have people waiting for me to return to Mount Roxby. I may not be an alpha to a large pride like my father but I do still have a pride. One that needs me.

"Look guys, this is fun to watch and all, but if we have walked into a trap, don't you think we should make a move?" Matt says, and as much as I can't stand the guy I'll give him props for choosing his words wisely. No orders hiding there.

With one last determined stare, I drop eye contact with Sassy and find myself hoping she doesn't do something stupid that will get us both killed tonight.

I knew if they took me I could wait out whatever they put me through until Dad calls in the cavalry, but if they get Sassy and I see them doing things to her…I'm not sure I'd be able to keep my cool.

It might end up being me who gets us killed.

"Matt's right. We need to get what information we can and get back to the pride so we can make a plan of attack."

After a quick glance around I come up with our next movements because we're sitting ducks and need to get out of the firing line before they realise we're here. The more I think about it, the more I wonder if we managed to stop before we set off whatever intruder alarm system they have.

I pin Matt and Will with a long hard stare. "You guys walk twenty metres east before you head back in the direction of the warehouse and be sure to watch every step you take."

They both nod in acknowledgement.

"Sass and I will stay on this trail." All three of them look at me, concern clear on their faces. I wave them off. "For all we know we could have set off a silent alarm already. Sass and I can at least play a happy couple on a romantic walk if we get some company."

Sassy gives me a look of disbelief. "In the middle of nowhere? They'll never believe that."

I step up close, sliding my arm over her shoulder and slip my fingertips into the arse pocket of her shorts. Shorts that I'd noticed hug her curves delightfully. "Sure they will, sweet cheeks." I squeeze her arse through her pocket, emphasising the name as I plant a kiss against her temple as if it's something I'd done a thousand times before.

A slow rumbling sound leaves her throat but she doesn't pull away. Instead she leans into me and slides her hand up my chest, her energy sending shivers across my skin and causing my lion to stir. "I just love it when we get to play like this, Snookums."

My heart sinks at the nickname but I try not to show it outwardly because, knowing Saskia, if I show any kind of reaction to the name she'll never give it up.

Being so close to her and having her scent overpowering my senses feels surprisingly right and it's in this moment I know I've started a game I never intended on playing. A dangerous one.

Matt chuckles as he and Will walk away, and I can only imagine the stories they're going tell back at the pride.

———

AS THE WAREHOUSE comes into sight we drop into a crouch, immediately forgetting the couple act.

No one had approached us on our journey so either we hadn't set off any alarms or we'd wrongly guessed that the trail was a trap.

Seeing an opening to the left I point towards it, indicating that's where we'll head. With finger gestures I direct her to go straight to the outer wall from where we are now and make her way to the opening along that. I also let her know with the same style of finger movements that I'll go along the tree line, past the opening, and come at it from the other side. After she gives me a silent nod we both run off.

The night is quiet, and it makes me wonder whether we'd been given bad information because surely if this was a headquarters of some kind there would be more noise than we can hear right now.

A twig snaps beneath my feet causing me to pause and brace myself for the sound being overly loud in the silent night. Only there isn't a sound. No sound at all.

I glance down at the twig and see the snapped piece beneath my feet. I frown, knowing it should have made a noise. My gut tells me something isn't right, and I purse my lips and let out a whistle to warn Saskia, only to find although my mouth did the motion, the sound didn't pierce the silent night.

I watch Saskia press herself against the tin wall of the warehouse, not taking her eyes off the opening to her right and definitely not acknowledging my attempt at getting her attention.

Magic!

It's nothing more than a thought, but the second it hits my mind I realise we were stupid not to notice it earlier. There should be so many noises of the night filling the air and we just walked right in with nothing but pure silence.

Fuck!

I can't even think when it started. I'd not even tried to verbalise the directions to Saskia and, once the warehouse had come into sight, we'd been so focused on the building coming closer that we'd not considered talking to each other. We were in hunt mode and hunting is best done in silence.

It shouldn't be a surprise to learn there's magic being used since we know they'd been using some kind of magic to hide their tracks back in pride territory. I could kick myself for letting that piece of information slip my mind.

Hoping there are no spells or wards that will ruin our chances of recon I dash for the side of the warehouse, my eyes flitting across our surroundings, looking for any sign of attack and seeing no movement except Sassy's figure creeping closer to the opening.

Half a metre from the wall I'm overwhelmed with noises. Shaking my head, I try to focus on individual sounds in an effort to fight the abrupt onslaught of noise. I keep up my pace, only pausing as I lean against the cold metal wall of the warehouse roughly a metre from the opening.

I lock eyes with Saskia, who is almost the same distance away from the other side of the opening, as I try to count the voices I can hear. It's impossible, there are too many. It confirms that we've definitely found their headquarters.

Sassy points to herself and then the opening, clearly suggesting she should go inside. I shake my head, no, but she slips inside without even looking for my response.

I want to lurch forward and drag her back but my lion forces me to go with it. To trust her to look out for herself and not take any risks that could lead her into fatal danger. My human side wants to argue walking into a warehouse packed with the enemy is pretty much walking straight into danger, but I also get the reasons for not grabbing her. It wouldn't be quiet and we'd draw attention. We're meant to be sneaking in, finding out what information we can, before heading home and coming up with a plan of attack.

I slip inside and use some storage shelves to my left as cover. Looking through gaps between the boxes I see a large open area that looks to be split into three sections.

There's a sleeping area made up of canvas camp beds set in rows, pillows and blankets neatly folded on top. A dining area is made up of plastic tables and chairs, which is currently bustling with people tucking into plates full of food. A rough head count gives me forty of the enemy. The majority of them have weapons visibly holstered at their waists or underarms which confirms they are certainly who we are looking for. The third section is at the far right side and partially hidden behind a screen of some kind. Knowing Saskia has gone that way I'm confident she'll check that out thoroughly so we can come up with an accurate headcount.

I focus my attention on watching the people in front of me and gathering whatever information I can from their scattered conversations.

———

AFTER WE'D ARRIVED home and filled Dad in on all the information we gathered about the Cleaners, he decided a pride meeting was needed. We had to come up with a plan and, since the pride's safety was at stake, he wanted everyone involved in the decision.

It's strange walking into the arena after my time away. The red dirt beneath my feet had seen plenty of deaths over the years, a lot of them by my hand—but that isn't why we're here today.

As I glance around at the people gathering this morning, I'm surprised to see even the full human members are standing with their lion family members. The Quilpie Pride has always felt the human members to be less important, the shifters of the family being far more superior to them. It doesn't mean each and every family member isn't loved equally because they are; it's just that the humans' opinion on pride matters don't count. They aren't the ones that fight, so they have nothing of value to offer and shouldn't be involved in those dealings. It's an archaic way of thinking and seeing the fact that my father invited *everyone* makes me think he's finally trying to pull us out of that.

A wave of pride fills me as I watch him talking to a

family by the entrance. As much as he wants me to step into his shoes and take over, I think he's doing a fine job himself and I know he's got plenty of years as alpha left in him yet. Even if *he* doesn't feel it.

Once people stop trickling in Dad steps into the middle of the arena and clears his throat before speaking. "I want to start off by saying thank you to each and everyone of you for coming."

A few whispers run around the crowd but I can't distinguish any words.

Dad dismisses the whispers with a wave of his hand. "I can tell a lot of you have questions so I'll get straight to the point about why I've gathered you all here this morning. As you are all well aware we've been under attack by a group of Cleaners. Jared and a handful of other pride members spent all of yesterday hunting them down."

All eyes turn to me. I take a step forward to join my father in the centre, offering a smile here and there.

Dad pats me on the shoulder as I come to a stop beside him and he eyes the crowd as he forges on. "A couple of our attackers were killed, but those that weren't led us to a warehouse which looks to be a large living and training centre of theirs'."

"What are we waiting for? We should be attacking them," one of the guys calls out. As I glance around to find the culprit, I notice a number of others nodding in agreement.

Dad clears his throat. "That is why I've gathered you here. The numbers they have, not to mention weapons, means we would be slaughtered if we attacked—even if we manage to surprise them."

A rumble runs around the crowd as friends mutter between themselves.

"This isn't just our fight. They have prisoners." He lets

out a low whistle and Mum walks in with Little Tiger at her side.

I can't contain my warning growl as people start to step forward to get a closer look. Rage flows through me; I had no idea he was planning to parade her around like this. Mum stops at Dad's other side and gives me an apologetic look. Little Tiger struts past Dad like she doesn't have a couple of hundred hostile strangers staring at her, coming to a stop when she reaches my side. Her fur brushing against my bare calf manages to settle my lion down a little.

"They don't care about species, they only care that we aren't human. That we're different from them. We need to come together with other species because we need to form an army and wipe them out. There's no place for prejudices when we're being attacked for the same reasons."

I brace myself as I understand where he's going with this. After all, it was my suggestion to him last night, I just never thought he'd bring it up with the pride. They're going to hate it, even if they see that it's the only way.

"After this meeting I'm going to request that Jared contacts the Alpha of the Mount Roxby Pack. The pack he's been living amongst. The pack he's been protecting a member and her pup for. They are his allies—"

"They are my friends," I say, cutting him short.

Dad gives me an apologetic nod and waves his hand to offer me the floor.

I hadn't planned on saying anything. I was just here to offer my father support. To stand strong as a unit.

As I flick my eyes around the crowd and take in the defensive stances of the majority—arms crossed over their chests and fixed stares. Taking a deep breath, I tell my lion to stand down no matter what anyone says. They need to see that I'm on their side and no one elses. "The wolves will be more than happy to join us in this fight."

Feeling Little Tiger leaning against my leg I decide she is my best point to run with. "This Tasmanian Tiger cub was chained, with silver spikes digging into her flesh where the collar sat. They were torturing her and she's only a cub. She doesn't deserve that."

She nudges at the tips of my fingers and I sink them into the fur on her head, giving her a good scratch behind her ears before carrying on. "She hasn't shifted since we found her and that is okay, she can take as long as she needs to be able to trust us. And you guys have that right, too. You don't have to trust the wolves or any other species we may call in. But please, have trust in my father. *Our* alpha. He will not put you and your families in danger, because at the end of the day, we are all one family. We are pride."

Everyone doesn't instantly agree like I'd hoped. Realistically I knew that would never have happened. It would have been too easy. Instead, people start talking over one another. The main question being thrown around is why my word should be trusted.

I'm left wondering that perhaps my being here and speaking up wasn't such a good idea after all.

15

HYSTERICAL CONFESSIONS

SASKIA

"LOOK, I know you don't like the idea of the wolves coming into our territory but they aren't the enemy," Grigori shouts over the raised bickering voices. "Jared has been living with them and he vouches for them. They can help us bring down these Cleaners."

Becky nudges me in the ribs. "You've been hanging out with Jared. Should his word be trusted?" The crowd around me falls silent as though they're waiting to hear my answer.

Glancing across the space, I allow my eyes to fall on Jared before scanning the crowd, trying to connect with everyone in the room. Wanting them to see the truth in my words. I nod. "A hundred percent. He may be aligned with the wolf pack, but he's always wanted what is best for us. He left his new home, and the wolf and newborn pup he'd been protecting, the minute the pride called. What more do you guys need from him to prove the pride comes first?"

There's chatter back and forth throughout the crowd before one of the older female pride members speaks up. "Bringing the wolves in is smart idea. We need the help. We've lost too many of our own lately." I roll my eyes—she only wants the wolves so they can die fighting instead of our people.

Agreement runs through the crowd like wildfire and Grigori speaks up. "I appreciate your acceptance and I hope we can give the wolves a warm welcome when they arrive."

"Don't push it, Grigori. We won't eat them. That'll have to be enough." Grigori's beta, Mitchell, jumps in. Grigori laughs raucously and I can't help but cringe a little. I don't think Mitchell was joking. The lions despise other species, does he not remember how Bel was treated once she became an adult? The thought of her makes me wonder if she'll be one of those that come to help. I really hope she doesn't. I don't think anyone will be able to look past any old memories that the sight of her may induce.

Many pride members died trying to kill her. Many even at Jared's hand, it's only because he was doing it out of protection that people don't hold it against him.

Becky drags me away from the crowd and, knowing the discussion is over, I follow without argument. She opens the door to her little studio apartment at the back of Mrs Beecham's house and heads straight for the fridge. "I've got a bottle of wine in here. We need a good girly chat."

Resigning myself to the Spanish inquisition that I know is coming, I pull out a stool from under the island bench and prop myself on it.

"Don't look at me like that. If the shoe was on the other foot, you'd be dying to ask all the questions I am." I roll my eyes but don't bother arguing as she screws the top off a bottle and fills two glasses with golden liquid. She's right, I'd have pinned her down for questions well before now. "You used to hate the guy and now you're looking at him all gooey eyed and singing his praises in front of the pride. What gives?"

Taking my time to mull over my answer, I have a sip of the wine, closing my eyes as the familiar taste of my favourite washes over my tongue. "I do not look at him gooey eyed." I sigh. "But...I was wrong about him before. I, like most people, thought he was killing pride members for the likes of a wolf, but he wasn't. Bel was never a *wolf* to him, she was someone weaker, someone who wasn't being treated fairly. She needed a protector and that's exactly what he gave her."

Becky's forehead creases as she thinks about my words. "I still don't get it."

I shake my head. "I don't know…" I struggle to find a way to explain what's going through my mind. "He's an alpha. He's born to protect those weaker than him. I didn't understand until I saw him with the wolf and her newborn." Seeing her confused look tells me I didn't manage to clear it up. One day, they'll see what I do. They'll see right through his power and strength to the core of him, to his heart. His big, protective, caring heart.

"You're blushing." Becky giggles.

Knowing I'm in trouble I try to distract her with the man she's had her eye on for a long time. "So, have you jumped Mitchell yet?"

"Get stuffed, Sass. You know I'm not the kind to jump guys." She bats at me before taking a large swig of her wine.

I know she isn't, but seeing her drink that wine with gusto makes me think she's trying to hide something. I grab the bottle and hold it out of her reach. "Tell me what happened or you won't get a top up."

"Some best friend you are!" She huffs. "You're not playing fair at all."

Quirking a brow, I give her a no-nonsense look, eliciting a roll of her eyes.

"Fine. But you better not laugh."

I give her a mock salute. "Scout's honour."

Becky sighs. "You and I both know you weren't a scout." She gives her glass a meaningful look and I top her up. "My lioness jumped him."

My hand moves to my mouth and it takes everything I have to suppress my laugh.

"At the hunt in front of the whole pride," she finishes.

I can no longer do it and if that means I'm a terrible best friend I'll take it. My laugh bursts free from my pressed lips. I laugh and laugh until my sides hurt.

"Oh, Becky." I look at her with sympathy in my tear filled eyes. I've not cried from laughing in such a long time. It's kind of refreshing to be so carefree. But I do understand her dilemma.

You can easily play the emotional, tipsy—providing you can get enough hard liquor in you—and even confused card if it's your human side that does the jumping. Your animal form though? Those excuses will not fly. She only does things on basic instinct. She fucked him because she wanted to. It was no mistake. The fact that she did it in front of the pride means she wanted everyone to know about it. Make her claim.

"Did you actually fuck or did she just try?" I ask, not knowing which answer I'd prefer her to come out with. One would be bad; the other would be very bad.

"We fucked like we'd been living in a monastery." She buries her head in her hands and lets out a groan of embarrassment. "And no, he hasn't tried a repeat." Becky lifts her head and grabs her glass. "In fact, he's tried his hardest to stay away from me. Today was the first time we'd been in the same space as each other and, if you didn't notice, he was careful to keep as much distance between us as possible by staying right across the other side of the arena."

I think back and realise she's right. "What the fuck? He needs his head kicking in." I jump up, ready to go find the dickhead and give him a piece of my mind, when Becky grabs my arm and tugs me back in my seat.

"No! If he isn't man enough to claim me then I don't want him. Am I hurt? Yes. But I'll get over it."

I relax in my seat and she releases my arm. I don't agree with her but if that's how she feels I have no right to jump in.

Although I can't guarantee I won't discreetly quiz him about it if the opportunity arises—and I'm certain it will.

———

AFTER A COUPLE of hours of talking shit and drinking good wine we decide to binge watch some episodes of Gracie and Frankie on Netflix. We love those two ladies and often joke that, that'll be us in the future, just without the gay ex-husbands.

"You know you can always have the couch," Becky offers as she places both of our glasses into the sink.

I screw up our wrappers from the burger bar down the road and throw them in the bin. "No, I'm feeling a little twitchy. I think I need a run." My skin shivers at the thought and I know it's the right decision. My lioness wants out.

Becky walks me to the door and we hug goodbye. Knowing Jared was going to call the wolves earlier means, providing they agree to fight along side us, they'll probably be arriving tomorrow sometime and then we'll make our move the next day, so I don't offer to make any plans. I've seen that place and the people they held captive and still have. There is no way I'm not being involved in taking them down.

The sun's setting as I walk towards the bushland, and a silhouette coming out of the tree line heads in my direction.

"Saskia," Mitchell greets me with a nod.

Just the man I wanted to see. My inner-self is practically rubbing her hands together in glee. "Mitchell." I nod. "I heard I missed out on quite the show during the last hunt."

"I don't know what you've heard bu—"

I cut him off. "Don't bullshit me, Mitch. Becky and me have been best mates since we were in nappies. You hurt her and you have me to deal with. That shouldn't surprise you."

Mitch takes a deep breath and releases it. "Yeah. I know." He doesn't elaborate so I decide to prod him a little.

"So, what's going on? Why haven't you claimed her?"

He runs a hand through his hair and points out a park bench up the road. "Do you wanna sit?"

"No, I'm feeling twitchy. I wouldn't be able to sit still if I tried," I say as I shake out my hands to aid in releasing some of the extra energy I have coursing through me.

"You need to run."

"I do. But I think you talking your thoughts through is more important right now." I've known Mitchell for a long time. He's a good guy, so I can't imagine him being a dick to Becky intentionally.

Mitch starts for the bench and I follow silently behind. I pause a few feet away and watch him pace back and forth behind it. "What happened at the hunt…it should have never gotten that far. I should have stopped it."

"Why? You think she isn't good enough for you? I'll have you know Bec—"

"No!" He cut me off. "Becky is…I'm not good enough for her. I'm much older than her."

I sigh and his eyes instantly fall on me. "We're shifters, Mitch. You know as well as I do that we don't look our age like humans do. We live long fucking lives. That's a shit excuse and you know it."

A loud crack has my head turning to see Mitchell shaking out his fist. I flick my eyes to the tree beside him, not at all surprised to see a crack running down the middle of its trunk.

"I'm Grigori's Second. People aren't going to make it easy for her if I claim her. There are a few who I know will try to fight her for it. I don't want her hurting." His words could be taken as a boast but the concern I can hear in the wobble of his voice made it clear he wasn't at all boasting.

"Becky can handle those bitches, but I'm not sure she can handle the hurt from your rejection. She's putting on a brave face now, but in the long run…" I shrug, hoping he understands what I'm saying.

Mitch rubs a hand over his face and releases a deep breath, his shoulders dropping in defeat. "You're right."

"Wait a minute." I dig around in my pocket and pull out my phone. "Say that again so I can record it. Next time someone questions my opinion I can play them that."

He lets out a laugh and I'm somewhat relieved to have broken the seriousness of the moment as I giggle along with him.

"Thanks, Saskia."

I give him a wide smile. "You're welcome. Now go and get your woman."

He starts walking in the direction I'd just come from.

"And don't forget…if you ever hurt her you'll have me to deal with," I remind him gently.

"Thanks for the warning, but it ain't gonna happen." He shouts over his shoulder as he quickens his pace, disappearing into the night.

I crack my neck and stride towards the bushland needing to run more than ever. Once I'm in the cover of the trees, I strip off my clothes, hanging them high up on a branch so they don't get too dirty.

Taking a deep calming breath I call my lioness forward as I give her the freedom to take control. I'm soon running through the trees, stretching my legs and taking in the night air.

As I inhale I catch a familiar scent and change direction, running at full speed towards it, feeling the sudden urge to reach it before anyone else.

I pounce over a high shrub and halt on the dirt covered

ground. The feeling of eyes on me tells me they're here. *Somewhere*.

I take in a deep breath as my eyes roam our surroundings trying to pinpoint where they may be hiding. It's in this moment that I realise the why scent is so familiar. It's a scent I'd been covered in for the last two days. *Jared's*.

My human half panics over the fact that we're both in our animal forms and they'll both scent Jared on me. It might mean something to their basic instincts. They might not understand the joke behind it all.

In an instant I shift, needing to be the one in control. "I know you're here, Jared,"

My lioness stays strong and right at the forefront of my consciousness, making it clear she'll take over control if I do something she isn't happy with.

16

REQUEST FOR HELP

MY HANDS SLIDE around Bel's waist as I brush my lips against the shell of her ear. "You know, we could sneak out of here, no one would even care."

Her warm laugh is like music to my ears. "We're hosting a party, I'm pretty sure people will notice if we disappear."

I place a kiss against her jaw and work my way down her neck with soft, gentle butterfly kisses.

Bel tilts her head to the side to give me more access and when she hums in pleasure I know I've won her over. She turns in my arms and runs her hands up my chest. "Where were you thinking of escaping to?" She pins me with a stare, her eyes full of mischief.

"How ab—"

My phone lets out an annoying buzz and I sigh as I reach into my pocket, pulling it out. Being pack alpha has its cons and being always accessible is one. Jared's name flashes on the screen and I smile as I answer.

"Jared. You need to work on your timing. You're becoming quite the cock blocker."

Jared lets out a hearty laugh and Bel chuckles beside me.

"Hey Bel,"

"How's the pride?" Bel asked, before carrying on. "Uncle Jack and Aunt Lily seemed okay when I spoke to them yesterday, although they didn't tell me much about what's happening. They never do." I rubbed my hand over her back to comfort her, knowing how deep her past with the pride cut her.

Jared sighed. "The Cleaners have a cell close by and they've been picking pride families off. They've got a Mage of some kind helping them out because there's been some spells being used to cover their tracks and block out sounds."

"Holy shit! What's Grigori got planned?" Bel asked. I was happy to sit back and let her ask the questions; after all, it was her family members who were in danger.

"A few of us went out and found a trail which led to warehouse that seems to be a headquarters of some kind. It was purely a recon mission, so we could know what we're up against. And it doesn't look good. They have prisoners. Shifters."

Bel pins me with a look and I worry about what's going through her mind.

"We found a Tasmanian Tiger cub, she had a spiked collar around her neck. Pulling those silver spikes out of her neck was the worst thing I've ever had to do. And I know they have more. Walking away from that warehouse and leaving the rest of the prisoners there was hard. The only thing that stopped me from charging in was that I knew we'd be slaughtered if we tried. The weapons they have…Silver bullets."

"What do you need?" I ask, knowing he hasn't just called to relay this information.

"Pack members. Whoever is willing to fight. We need numbers, Theo. It's not just lions they have, they don't care about—"

"Jared, we aren't like your pride. We don't need to be talked into helping others. If we can help and someone needs it, we'll do it. I'll make some calls to a couple of decent alphas I know who might be able to send some guys, too."

"Thank you."

I glance at my watch and make some quick calculations. "We'll be there in forty-eight hours. Is there anyone in particular you think might be useful?"

Jared lets out a sharp breath. "Billy ain't gonna like it… but Misty might be able to help out counteracting the wards the other mage is using."

I smirk, knowing he's right. Billy is going to hate it and Dominick is gonna hate it even more so. "You realise, Dominick will insist on being there too. How will the pride handle that?"

"Ruby, too." Bel adds.

I glare in her direction. "Over my dead body."

"Good luck trying to stop her." Jared mutters and I suddenly feel like denying him any help at all. "The pride understands what it's going to take to bring down this cell of Cleaners. Anyone who comes to help will be welcomed, no matter what species they are. Except…" he pauses, and I can hazard a guess at what his next words might be.

"Go on."

"Bel…You can't come."

"The fuck I can't! My family is there. Jared, you're not my protector anymore," Bel argues, her voice rising in anger.

The chatter in the other room disappears and I'm well aware they are all listening into our conversation. They may not be able to hear Jared through the thickness of the door but they'll hear Bel and me easily enough.

"I'm not trying to protect you, Bel. I'm trying to protect everyone. Including those prisoners having god only knows what done to them right now while they are still in the hands of the Cleaners." He takes a quick breath and carries on. "The pride is willing to accept that this affects all shifters and we need to work together to deal with the Cleaners. But I'm afraid that if you turn up, their anger and pain towards the losses they had in the past will blind them to the current situation. We need to be on the same side. Please, Bel."

The pain flits across Bel's face and her shoulders drop in defeat. "Okay."

"Okay?" Jared asks, his voice unsure, seemingly waiting for the other shoe to drop. I don't blame him, if I couldn't see Bel's demeanour with my own eyes I'd probably be thinking the same thing. Bel isn't one to give in easily.

"Just…You all better come back in one piece."

"We will. And we'll kick arse for you." I could hear the smile in Jared's voice, making me realise he'd been extremely worried about Bel's reaction. That had probably bothered him more than asking me for help.

"How's Alyssa? I tried calling her earlier but she didn't answer," Jared questions. "She feels content but with the distance I'm not sure how accurate it is."

I think back to the phone call I had a few hours ago and smile. "She's doing good. The person I have watching her checked in earlier. Both her and Lee are well."

His sigh rings down the line, bordering on a huff and I completely understand it. It's how I'd felt all those months when I was Alyssa's alpha but I couldn't do anything to help her. Jared will be feeling torn about helping his old pride and wanting to be with his new one.

"I'm going to drop in on her tomorrow. Hopefully get some baby cuddles. I'll call you afterwards and give you a detailed report," Bel offers, she slips her hand around my waist and I lift my arm to give her access to my side.

"Thanks, Bel. I love ya."

"Hey. We have a good alpha to alpha relationship here, don't be ruining that with love declarations to my mate."

Jared and Bel both laugh and I'm glad I managed to break the tension, even though part of me wasn't joking.

A tortured sounding animal's cry rings through the phone.

"Shh… It's alright Lil' Tiger. You're safe," Jared coos. "I've gotta go. See you soon, Theo. And thanks." The call disconnects before either of us can reply.

Bel presses a kiss to my collarbone. "You'll kill the bastards." It was a statement not a question, but I answered anyway.

"Painfully."

They deserve nothing less if that cub's cries are anything to go by.

17

AN ALLURING SCENT

JARED

I DISCONNECT the call and run my hand over Lil' Tiger's back, hoping the feel of my alpha power manages to calm her down. Her little body shakes beneath my hand and anger rises within me. A child should never have to feel such terror. Those men had done unspeakable things to her and I personally can't wait to have my own fun with them in return. After all, it's well known that cats like to play with their prey.

The thought of my lion puts an idea in my head and I quickly shift, not caring about my clothes as they rip or the extra pain it causes on my sensitive changing limbs.

I let out a small roar, to make Lil' Tiger aware that there's a larger predator in the room.

Her eyes pop open and she weighs me up, not blinking.

I shake out my mane and lay down on the floor, hoping my calm and simple movements let her know I'm not here to harm her.

The tension in her body seems to drift away as she once again relaxes into a curled up ball and closes her eyes. I watch and listen as her breathing slows, knowing exactly when she's once again drifted off to sleep.

I doze along side her for an hour or two before my lion gets restless, feeling a sudden overwhelming urge to run.

I mentally reach out to my father, who as an alpha can communicate with all his pride mates in their animal forms.

I need to run.

Go. I'll watch over the little one. His voice rings through my head.

No longer than a minute passes before the bedroom door pops open and I watch Dad step into the room and over to the chair by the window, his kindle in his hand. "I left the backdoor open," he breathes the words, clearly hoping they're quiet enough to not wake Little Tiger.

———

AS I STEP OUTSIDE a scent catches my lion's attention and he charges towards it without giving me a chance to place it. The stronger the scent becomes the slower he gets. Making it clear to me that he's hunting whoever this may be.

Crouching behind a bush, I spot the lioness through the leaves and the recognition of the scent finally clicks in my mind.

Sassy.

Of course he's chasing Saskia. After his actions the other day I shouldn't be the least bit surprised. He likes her and, honestly, so do I.

But we're not here to find a mate. We're here to help the pride and *leave*. We have people relying on us back in Mount Roxby.

Our own little pride.

Saskia's head tilts to the side like she's listening, and we stand frozen, trying not to alert her to our presence. She suddenly shifts, her golden lion changing into a five-foot-five blonde bombshell.

"I know you're here, Jared," she calls out.

My lion steps out of the bushes, his head held high proud that she recognised our scent. Knowing he can't communicate with her in his form he hands me control and I shift.

"You recognised my scent." The words are out before I even consider saying them and I belatedly realise my lion is still riding me.

"I've smelled nothing but your scent since you marked me. Of course I recognise it."

My lips lift into a smirk and I take a step towards her. She doesn't retreat and I take that as invitation to move closer still. As I come to a stop with barely an inch between us I lean forward and run my nose along her neck, breathing in my own scent against her skin.

Energy crackles between us, practically jumping from one of our limbs to the other's. The scent of arousal fills the air and it's in that moment I realise my dick is rock hard between us.

Our eyes connect, and I watch as Sassy's change from bright blue to coffee brown orbs before flicking back again, making it clear both human and lioness are with me. My eyesight shifts, my night vision becoming more defined and I know she's witnessing the same thing in my eyes.

My eyes drift to her mouth as she pulls her bottom lip between her teeth. Lifting my hand I cup her jaw and pull her lip free with the edge of my thumb. Unable to hold back, I crush my lips against hers in a passionate kiss.

Saskia's hands tug at my hips and I groan into her mouth as my bare cock comes in contact with her flesh. She lifts her leg and wraps it around my hips, clearly attempting to get some friction on her pussy.

Dropping my hand between us, I run my fingers over her slick heat, being sure to give her clit the attention she craves before sliding a finger inside.

"Jar… Ooh." She throws her head back in pleasure and I lean in, peppering her exposed neck with kisses.

I suck and gently bite at her neck loving the sounds it has her releasing. I add another finger to her pussy and pump them in a rhythm I know she'll enjoy. I wish I could be using my cock, but this isn't the place to have sex for the first time. No, for that I want to have her splayed out before me so I can devour every inch of her bare flesh.

"More. I need more Jar."

She's so close I could feel it in the erratic grinding of her hips. I couldn't give her the more she wanted, not here. We were already risking someone stumbling upon us and I didn't want anyone to see her in the throes of passion. It's something both my lion and I are in complete agreement with. No one will ever get to see her like this again. It's for our eyes only.

"I'm gonna have my cock in your pussy real soon, Sass. Is that what you want?" I whisper in her ear.

"Oh fuck, yes!"

My lips pull into smirk.

My sassy girl likes dirty talk. I file that piece of information away for future use. I can definitely work with that.

With my spare hand I pinch a nipple and within seconds I feel her walls clamping down on my fingers as Saskia cries out in pleasure. I press small butterfly kisses up her neck and along her jaw as she gains her composure.

Saskia drops her leg and takes a step back. I brace myself for a change of heart but the grin that graces her face as she locks eyes with me tells me that's not happening. "My turn."

Before I can even process what she might mean by those words, she drops to her knees before me. I open my mouth to complain about her kneeling in the dirt but, as her hand grips my cock and the tip of her tongue licks my length, all thoughts fall from my mind. I fist my hands at my sides to stop myself from sinking them in her hair and taking control.

Her tongue stops its delightful exploration. "Don't hold back."

My eyes pop open and lock on her glistening baby blues

pleading with me to do exactly as she asked. With a short sharp nod I relax, sinking my fingers into her short blonde tresses knowing that if I'm too rough she's more than strong enough to stop me in an instant.

Saskia engulfs my cock with her mouth and I can't hold in my guttural moan as the crown hits the back of her throat. "Fuck…Sass." Any chance of saying anything more disappears as the warmth of her mouth slides back up my length, causing my balls to draw up at the glorious sensation.

As much as I'd like this to last I know it's not going to happen. It's been a long time since I'd had a woman touch me like this and Saskia seems to know exactly how to push all my buttons.

Saskia cups my balls and gives them a gentle squeeze, bringing me to the point of no return. I come so quickly I don't even have a chance to warn her to pull off before I empty myself into her mouth.

Saskia moans as she swallows down everything I give her, making me think she wouldn't have pulled off even if I had warned her. She pulls back off my cock torturously slowly and gives her lips a slow lick clean, making me wish we were somewhere I could take this further.

I pull her against me as she stands, and take her mouth with mine, needing to kiss her. Surprisingly, enjoying the fact that I can taste myself on her. My lion's pleased she was marked with our seed. Anyone that comes in contact with her will know she's mine. Breaking the kiss I dip my head to press my lips to the crook of her neck. "My Sassy Girl," I state against her flesh, my voice rough with emotion as my lion comes to the surface.

"I don't remember agreeing to be your girl."

I hear the smile behind her words but can't hold back from sinking my teeth into her flesh, not hard enough to break the skin but more than enough to leave a mark. My lion's claiming her, and so am I.

"You agreed," I confirm. I lick over the bite hoping to soothe any pain it may have caused.

Saskia's light-hearted laugh eases my mind, making it clear she's on the same page as us.

"Where are your clothes?" I ask, suddenly feeling the need to have her dressed before anyone can see her nakedness. As shifters we see each other naked all the time but freshly satisfied with the scent of sex in the air is not how I want anyone to see her.

She grins. "Not far from Old Smithy's bench."

My heart sinks at her words. There isn't anywhere further away from where we are than the memorial bench that is Smithy's. I begrudgingly loosen my hold on her and step back. "Shift." I give her backside a quick pat to ease the seriousness of my command.

She screws up her face, making a show of thinking about it and a displeased rumble leaves my throat. She chuckles. "Fine, but this goes both ways. You have to shift too."

My skin ripples and I'm standing on all fours before her in no time. Giving her a questioning look with my lion's eyes.

She drops to her knees in front of me, her eyes being the only thing that shift making me aware that her lion is in control and using Saskia's form. Her hand sinks into my mane. "Mine," her lioness claims. She removes her hand from my fur as her limbs shift.

Using my alpha energy I reach out, pushing what power I can towards her hoping to make her shift easier and less painful. After all, this shift was because of me. I was the one that didn't want her naked. It's only fair that I'm the one to shoulder the burden.

Once her shift is completed I shake off the remaining

energy and her lioness's coffee brown eyes connect with mine as her voice rings in my head.

Thank you.

I let out a puff of air from my nose, letting her know it was nothing. My lion eases back onto his hind legs readying himself to pounce, deciding it's time to ease her mind with a little bit of playfulness.

Catching on quickly she bounds away before my paws even leave the ground and I'm suddenly running through the bushland chasing what my lion feels to be his mate.

Somewhere along the chase I manage to lose sight of Saskia but I'm not concerned because my keen sense of smell keeps me on her trail and I know it will lead me straight to her.

I slow my pace as I feel her energy change, being sure to give her a little privacy while she dresses. Stepping up to the edge of the tree line I expect to find her in the clearing ahead of me but all I can see is Old Smithy's bench looking deserted.

I scent the air with my tongue and know she's nearby. Dropping down into the long grasses around me, I use them as cover, and start to crawl to the right when something drops onto my back.

Saskia. Her scent and energy tells me as much.

On instinct I roll, taking Sass with me, careful not to crush her as I land on top of her. My paws pressed to the ground at either side of her head.

It reminds me of another time we were in this position, only days ago.

And it turns out my lion got what he wanted after all.

18

MIXED EMOTIONS

I WATCH Jared pace up and down Main Street waiting for the pack to arrive. They are supposed to be coming on a coach that the Mount Roxby Pack Alpha had hired.

I want to reach out and comfort him, try to distract him, but my lioness is urging me to stay back. She's right; Jared hasn't acknowledged what happened last night. And I'm left wondering if he's regretting it.

Even though he'd left me at the tree line not long after I'd jumped him, we'd left knowing things between us had changed. His lion once again covered me in his scent and this time I didn't mind in the slightest, because he was claiming me now, good and proper, even though we still had to be more physical to make our scents mix. He was also walking away covered in my scent, which pleased me to no end.

So yes, the fact that he hasn't so much as given me a wink today has me extremely worried. Especially because we've been around each other all day with other key members of the pride, coming up with a plan of attack for when the other fighters arrive.

Just as I decide to give in and approach Jared, a hand closes around my wrist. The person's scent is familiar but not quite right so I have no idea who it is until I turn to find my best friend, Becky. A broad smile plastered on her face.

"You look like that cat who got the cream," I point out, her smile so infectious I could feel it beaming.

"I don't know what you said to Mitch but I owe you the biggest thank you hamper on the planet."

At her mention of Mitch I suddenly realise why I didn't recognise her scent. It's mixed with Mitch's, meaning they've claimed each other as mates. I throw my arms around her and pull her into a warm embrace. "Congratulations, Becky. I'm so happy for you," I state into her hair.

She pulls back, holding me at arms length, her brow creased into a deep frown. "It smells like you've been busy too."

"Not as busy as you. Now tell me all about it," I demand, hoping to get the subject back onto her. "Well, not the finer details."

We both laugh and she tugs on my arm pulling me away from the others. They'd still be able to hear if they wanted to but out of politeness, if someone walks away to talk, we shut their conversations out in an effort to not eavesdrop.

She leant in close and dropped her voice. "He stormed in all growly and took me right there against the front door."

I turn to give her wide eyes. "Your front door is all glass."

"It's frosted." She shrugs like that makes all the difference.

I shake my head and turn towards Jared as a sudden popping sound has me on high alert.

My lioness sits to attention ready if she needs to be called upon. A blonde girl who looks to be in her late teens, seemingly having appeared out of nowhere, throws her arms around Jared's neck.

"Rubes. It's good to see you," Jared states as he embraces her just as enthusiastically as she does him.

My hands form fists at my sides and I try to swallow a possessive roar.

Both Jared and *Rubes* turn their eyes on me and I'm suddenly aware I'd failed. Jared's lips lift into a grin as he releases his hold on the girl.

"Hmm… that's interesting." She gives him a raised brow. "You've clearly been busy," she says before waving at me, a friendly smile on her face even though I know I'm looking anything but friendly. I get a flash of fangs and realise that must explain the unusual scent I'd picked up but not really focused on.

Vampire.

The rumbling sound of an engine catches our attention and we all watch as a coach drives towards us. It pulls to a stop and once the doors open people start stepping off.

I look wide-eyed from the growing crowd of strangers to Jared. I was expecting maybe ten or fifteen people. There are easily fifty men and women here.

A handsome guy with dark blonde hair is the last to get off and I recognise him instantly as The Alpha of the Mount Roxby Pride. He steps through the people and heads straight for Jared, a big smile on his face.

"Theo. Thanks for coming. It looks like you really did gather the troops." Jared weighs up the group of people and I suddenly realise he, too, was surprised by the turnout.

Theo winks. "We made a couple of stops on the way." He glances around before catching a guy's eye. "Ry."

There's an excited squeal that tears my eyes away from Ry and the handful of people following him to Theo and Jared. A red headed guy has his arms wrapped around Rubes, nuzzling at her neck.

"We've only been apart for a day."

He spins her in his arms and presses a quick kiss to her lips. "That's a day too long."

My lioness slinks back into hiding at the sight, no longer feeling concerned about the blonde being after what's ours.

"Saskia." Jared's voice pulls my attention back towards him and he waves me over. "Come and meet everyone, you know how many rooms everyone has spare."

He was right. I'd been put in charge of organising where everyone will be sleeping for the night since we won't be attacking until dusk tomorrow. It'll be good to meet everyone and get a feel for whom I could place where. Some of our pride members are uneasy about sharing living quarters with other species. Some so uneasy that they flat out declined to offer up the spare rooms they may have.

I step up to Jared and his hand falls on my shoulder. I know it's a claim, as do all the other shifters here, and it takes all my willpower not to shrug it off—he can't ignore me all day and then, the minute new faces arrive, stake his claim— but I won't make a fool of him in front of strangers. No, I'll hash it out with him later; in private.

"Sass, this is Theo, the Alpha of the Mount Roxby Pack," he introduces, with a wave of his hand towards the alpha.

"Nice to meet you again." Theo offers me his hand and I take it in a quick shake. "It's just a shame it's under such unfortunate circumstances."

"Yes," I agree. My eyes flick to the couple beside him who are giving me an intense look.

He clears his throat and starts the introductions. "This is Ryan, Beta of the Falls Creek Pack, and his mate Harriet."

"And Enforcer of the Falls Creek Pack," she states giving Theo a glare. "It's two thousand and nineteen, surely women can be introduced by their pack positions too."

"My apologies Harriet, my mate would have my balls for that. But she'd also have them for not pointing out a mate claim too."

When Harriet gives him a smile he moves onto a tall guy with a shaved head, dressed in bike leathers. He has a raven-haired female tucked into his side. "My enforcer, Billy, and his mate, Misty, she isn't the pack witch as such but that is the capacity in which she is here."

A popping sound fills the air and a tall man with dark shoulder length curls appears behind the couple.

"And right on cue this is Dominick, Vampire King of Mount Roxby, and their other mate."

"Lucky woman," I state as I give the nervous female a grin.

Jared's hand tightens on my shoulder and I turn to face him, a glare plastered on my face. "Yes?"

His eyes flash golden. "Not sharing."

I sigh dramatically. "Fun spoiler."

Harriet laughs. "Oh, I like you. We should definitely be friends."

"Do all Vampires pop like that?" I hear Becky whisper, as would've everyone else.

"Only the special ones," Dominick states. There is a superior air to him and I can tell by that alone that he's an old one. Then again you wouldn't become King without being around for a long time.

"We have another group on the way from the Rossi Pack in Western Australia. They should be arriving within the hour," Theo says in a tone that seems to command our attention back to him.

———

IT TAKES a good hour to get everyone introduced to their host families and settled into their rooms. Just in time for the next smaller group to arrive. They pull up in a seven seater SUV and Theo welcomes them with friendly hugs all around.

It amazes me how the different packs can be so friendly

with each other. alphas, hell, all dominant animals, are territorial and protective. They should see each other as a threat. It seems to go against their instincts.

"How can you all get along so well?" The question falls out of my mouth before I can stop it, and I can't help but feel a little dumb to ask such a basic question as all eyes fall on me, and I feel my face heat.

Jared takes my hand in his and comfortingly rubs his thumb over my skin there. His energy relaxes my uneasiness instantly. "It took me a while to get my head around it when I first arrived in Mount Roxby and Theo was happy to welcome me into his town. Some days I still don't get it when I really think about what our natural instincts should be, but my lion is at ease around him and his pack so that's what I go with."

"Our animals may want to initially view each other as a threat but our human counterparts can see how we can be allies and even friends. Like how we're coming together now to fight with each other against a common enemy," Jesse, the Alpha of the Rossi Pack, states before glancing at his quiet mate beside him. "Theo's brother, Cain, brought my mate back to me when I couldn't find her. I owe him everything. It helped me see that even though there are bad alphas and packs out there, like the one that had taken her initially, there are also guys like Cain out there."

"It's good to know there are people who have your back when you need them," Jesse's mate says, her voice gentle and yet demanding.

Their words are like a seed of hope. Maybe this visit will do more for the pride than just stop more of us dying at the hands of the bounty hunters. Maybe we can grow and see that having connections to others is a good thing.

"Jared, now that we are all here, is there somewhere we

could go to run. I'm certain most of our wolves will be feeling a little restless after our long journey here."

Jared drops my hand and runs his fingers through his hair. A gesture I've noticed him do a lot since he arrived. "I'm so sorry, Theo. Of course, I should have thought about that sooner." He flicks his eyes to me and the concern in them isn't hard to see.

"The bushland around our little town is all our territory and you are more than welcome to run freely. The borders were freshly marked last night so you shouldn't have any problems staying safe from prying eyes. Even if you do go outside of our land, our closest neighbours are a long way off so there are no real risks anyway." The wolves nod and I carry on. "We do have enforcers on patrol at various points along the border, keeping an eye out for The Cleaners. They are aware you'll be arriving and are under strict orders not to attack any wolves that they come across. The rest of the pride will be staying in their human forms until they've been introduced to you all to reduce the risk of any misinterpreted threats."

"That is much appreciated, Saskia. Thank you." Theo gives me a grateful smile and I feel myself smiling back.

Seeing how welcoming these people are to others, I can understand why Jared settled into Mount Roxby so easily.

As the wolves head off for their run I expect Jared to join them but he hangs around until we're the only two left standing by the edge of the road. I watch as he turns his attention from the retreating wolves to me. He steps in close and brushes my loose hair behind my ear, an excited gleam in his eyes.

"I've finally got you to myself."

Part of me wants to take a step back—show him how pissed I am—but I can't, not when his breath blows over my flesh as he presses a kiss to my forehead.

"So you do want me to yourself then?"

He pulls back and I can easily see the crease in his brow. "All day long. What makes you think different? Because you clearly do."

I rub at his frown with my thumb and shake my head, dismissing it. "It doesn't matter. N—"

"It does matter," he states cutting me off. "I've hurt you and I didn't even notice. Please tell me." The look he gives me matches his pleading tone and, seeing that he genuinely didn't realise what he'd been doing today, eases the pain I'd been hiding behind my anger.

"You've acted just like you usually do and it made me think that you regretted what happened between us."

Jared sighs. "I'm sorry, Sass." He tugs me against him and I slide my arms around his waist, enjoying being so close with him. "I've wanted nothing more than to pull you against me all day but, knowing how independent and sassy you are, I held back. Not wanting to put you in a position you weren't comfortable with in front of the pride's prying eyes."

The fact that he'd tried to put my feelings first makes me fall just a little bit more than I already have while getting to know him over the last few days. "Thank you for thinking of me like that, but next time just do what you feel, regardless of how I'll react. I know you can handle my sass."

He cradles my face with his hands, tilting it up towards him and he leans in, stopping only a breath away. "I love your sass. You're my Sassy Girl."

I nip at his lips. "I like the sound of that."

Jared rubs a thumb over my heated cheeks and I turn my face hoping to hide them.

"Don't." He tilts my face back towards him. "The blush looks good on you."

Needing to stop him looking at me so intently, I crush my mouth against his in a messy kiss. His scent permeates the air around us and I find my hands wandering up his back and over his shoulders to his chest. I'm desperate to explore his body but this isn't enough. I need flesh on flesh.

Jared stills my hands as he breaks the kiss. "Are you sure you're ready for this?"

I've never understood the need to mate. To have another claim you, possess you. But now, I want nothing more than to have Jared *own* me body and soul.

Hell, I crave it.

Stepping back out of his hold, I decide the best way to answer is to show him. Disappointment flashes in his eyes for a brief moment before I grab his hand and tug him down the street towards my home.

Jared pauses at the door as he closes it behind us and by the energy I can feel coming off him, I can easily guess he's trying to compose himself.

My little apartment is dark and quiet so I wander through the space and switch on a couple of side lamps, which give the room a nice soft glow before pulling out my phone and connecting my playlist to the wireless speaker on the kitchen bench top.

Gentle hands slide around my waist as Sam Smith croons to us. Soft fingertips slip under the edge of my tank top and I suck in a breath as they brush over the lace of my bra.

I tilt my head to the side giving Jared more access as he presses a kiss to my neck and his hands slide around my ribs to my back.

"I like that you're making it all romantic for us." Jared's voice is teasing and I can feel the smile on his lips as he presses another kiss, this time to my shoulder. His nimble fingers brush against my flesh sending shivers up my spine as he works at the fastening on my bra.

I'm too turned on to care about being embarrassed but I

still can't stop myself from denying it. "I wasn't being romantic, I just hate the quiet."

Jared lifts my top over my head and my bra easily comes off with it. He spins me around to face him, his eyes zeroing in on my breasts, the attention and hungry look in his eyes cause my nipples to pebble. "I've got you pegged. You're hiding a sweet romantic under all that sass."

His fingers brush over my nipples and I close my eyes on a moan. "Mmm…maybe you're right."

Jared chuckles. "I think you'd agree with anything I say if I keep doing this."

"Right again."

I bite at my lip as he dips down and runs a tongue around my nipple. Opening my eyes I watch as he switches over giving the other breast the same attention, his eyes on mine the whole time. They flash to gold and his teeth nip at the flesh.

His lion saying hello.

His tongue flicks out and soothes the sting of the bite.

Overwhelmed with arousal I tug at his shirt. "You need to get naked."

19

A HEALTHY CHALLENGE

JARED

I DON'T NEED to be told twice.

Grabbing the back of my shirt I pull it over my head. The scent of Sassy's arousal heady in the air spurs me on to tug down my shorts and boxers in one move.

Saskia reaches for the buttons on her denim shorts and I quickly still her hands. Her eyes lock with mine questioningly.

"Let me."

A small smile graces her face and she lifts her hands in surrender. "Make it quick, I don't need anymore foreplay."

I can't help but grin. "I haven't even started yet Sassy Girl."

"I swear to God, Jared. If you drag this out…"

She leaves the threat hanging and I kiss her pretty pouting lips. Her hands roam over my chest and once again I still them.

"Claim me." If her words don't get me moving, her pleading tone does.

My fingers work at the buttons on her shorts as I walk her backwards towards to the bed.

Saskia shimmies out of them before climbing on the bed and shifting back until her head is level with the pillows and she's resting on her elbows watching me.

"Well, what are you waiting for?"

"Let me soak in the magnificent sight before me. Just for a minute."

Her hand trails over her collar bone and lazily around one nipple. "There'll be plenty more times you'll get to soak in this sight. But right now…I need you to claim me."

A roar escapes my mouth as I climb over the bed and come to a stop, hovering over the beauty that's about to be mine forever. "Mine," I growl.

"Prove it."

Slipping my hand between us I glide my fingers over her wet folds and, seeing that she's more than ready, I guide the head of my cock to her entrance.

Our eyes never part as I sink into her warmth and once I'm fully seated I pause, giving us both a moment to adjust.

Saskia squirms beneath me clearly not needing the time. The keening noise she makes has me moving in an instant. I want to hear more of her noises. I want to have them imprinted in my mind—each and every one of them.

Her nails dig into my biceps and, by the stinging pain I can feel, I know she's broken the skin. I pull back and thrust harder, loving every pleasure-filled sound she releases.

Our movements become frantic and my thrusts are out of rhythm, but neither of us seems to care. My climax is getting closer and I can tell Sass is the same.

My lion's energy pulses over my skin and within seconds I feel Saskia's join it. I can see her lioness in her eyes and as she opens her mouth on a moan I catch sight of her teeth—not quite her lioness's but definitely not human either.

My balls draw up but before I allow my release I need my girl to come. Leaning forward, I whisper in her ear. "Come, Mate." I end the sentence by sinking my teeth into the flesh of her shoulder.

Her walls squeeze my cock as she screams in pleasure. I

lick at the bite soothingly, my thrusts not changing tempo in the slightest.

She shifts her head to lock her eyes with mine. "Mate."

The word leaves her lips before she draws back and sinks her teeth into my pec, directly over my heart.

"*Fuuuuck!*" I groan as I finally release my climax, her walls squeezing me anew.

Before I lose all control of my limbs I let myself roll to the side so that I'm not crushing Sass. She shifts with me and I pull her against my chest, liking being close to her.

As I start to come out of the post coital haze I recognise a shift inside me, not the pride bonds but something else.

Something deeper.

"Do you feel that?" Saskia asks, wonder in her voice.

"Our mate bond."

————

I FLICK my tongue over Saskia's clit, enjoying feeling her squirming beneath me. My phone starts vibrating but I ignore it, choosing to keep up my merciless teasing.

Saskia huffs in frustration. "Whoever that is, they're persistent. You should probably answer it. That's the sixth time they've called now and I don't think they're gonna give up."

"They'll have to wait. I'm busy making my mate come at the moment." Slicking a finger up I let it join my tongue aiming to do exactly what I'd just said I would.

Saskia releases a groan as she lays her head back on the pillow clearly enjoying my ministrations enough to ignore the incessant buzzing.

After a good amount of teasing and bringing her to the brink, I pick up my pace to ensure she finally reaches her climax.

"Yes…Jar… right there."

I didn't need her instruction her body was telling me more than enough but hearing her shorten my name and in that breathy voice has me turned on once again.

Part of me wishes we'd claimed each other sooner because we could have been enjoying each other like this for years. But knowing that we aren't like the wolves, in that we don't have true mates, because our females need to find their mate worthy for them to claim them and that makes me happy that we are wired that way.

While Sass recovers I work my way up the bed and lay on my back on the pillow beside her, lifting my arm when she makes a move to snuggle up to me.

Saskia's fingers draw patterns on my chest and I purr in pleasure.

"Did you just purr?" she asks with a giggle.

In the blink of an eye I roll us over so she's on her back and I'm hovering over her. "I'm pretty sure I could entice a purr out of you, too."

"Maybe when I'm in lion form, but it won't happen when I'm human."

I narrow my eyes. "Challenge accepted."

She pouts in return probably knowing there is no way of talking me out of it. Leaning down I nip at her lips.

My phone buzzes once again and I break the kiss with a groan, leaning my forehead against Sassy's. "I guess I should see who that is."

"Yes. It might be Alyssa." The way her tone changes on Alyssa's name makes me think there's an issue there, but from what I understand of Saskia she's pretty outspoken so there's no need for me to question her about it. She'll either work through it herself or bring it up and hash it out with me when she's ready.

Taking a moment, I focus on the pride bonds and feel for Alyssa. She feels surprisingly content and I tell Saskia that.

"She's not normally content?"

"No." I frown, suddenly concerned. "Since she lost her mate she's been empty and sad, with some very brief moments of happiness, but never content."

Saskia pushes at my chest. "Go. Answer it. If it isn't Alyssa, ease your mind and call her."

Giving her a grateful smile I press a quick kiss against her lips before slipping off the bed and grabbing my phone out of my discarded jeans.

There are a number of names in the list of missed calls on the screen and not one of them are Alyssa. Before I can even read through them all, Ruby's name flashes on the screen and I hit accept.

"This better be important."

A chorus of loud laughs ring through the phone and I pull the phone away from my ear slightly as I look over my shoulder and lock eyes with Saskia's, catching sight of her lips turning up into an amused smile.

"You love me. Admit it," Ruby teases.

"You're the annoying little sister I never had."

"If that isn't a love declaration, I don't know what is," Theo says with a chuckle.

There's a rustling on the bed and I feel Sassy press a kiss against my shoulder blade.

"Well, if you guys didn't want anything in particular…I've got something I could be doing here." I grumble suddenly feeling the urge to end the call and get back to my mate.

Raucous laugher fills the air. "Guys…*Seriously*?" Ruby huffs. "Jared, we're having a little get-together in the… What's this place called?"

No one seems to answer her, so knowing this town only

has one place worthy enough to host a get-together, I do. "The Mane Shed."

"That's it. Anyway, get your miserable arse here and bring the pretty lioness with you. I want to get to know the woman who's managed to win your heart…and soul."

"We'll be there soon." I hang up and turn to face Saskia who is kneeling on the bed, naked. It's a nice change from the girls I'm used to dating who are quick to hide themselves the minute the main act is over.

Being a shifter may mean we have to become fairly comfortable being in our birthday suits around others, but it doesn't mean when we're with a lover, and they're focused on our bodies, that we don't feel insecure about ourselves.

I rest my hands on her hips as she slides hers up my chest and around my neck. "I guess we'll have to show our faces. You're the one who has brought us together after all. If any pride members are there they'll feel better seeing you at ease with the strangers."

"You're right." I press a kiss to the tip of her nose and she screws it up reflexively. My heart expands as I take in this cute version of her. I have a feeling not many people get to see her like this—she's always seemed to be serious and determined.

"Get this fine arse covered up," I say as I give it a playful pat, making sure we get moving before I change my mind about going out altogether.

———

AS A SOFT WHIMPER floats through the air waking me up from my light sleep. I shift on the bed and walk over to the small bundle of blankets in the corner of the room, grateful that Sassy suggested we sleep at my parents' house.

"It's alright, Lil' Tiger. You're safe," I state quietly before running my hand over her head, being careful of the wounds from the silver collar that are taking their time to heal. I dread to think about the scars they'll leave behind when she's in her human form.

Her eyes pop open and she shudders, another whimper escaping before she nuzzles at my hand.

"Is everything okay?" Sassy asks, her voice raspy with sleep.

"Yeah, Sassy Girl. You go back to sleep." Sass grumbles something incomprehensible as I hear the covers rustle, alerting me to the fact that she's settling back down once again.

Little Tiger's stomach lets out a loud grumble and I roll my eyes as I check the time on my watch, two in the morning. "Come on then, lets get you a snack."

In the kitchen I pull a couple of steaks from the fridge and offer one of them to the little one. "Do you want them cooked or are they good like this?" I ask, not knowing who exactly is in control right now. Usually if it's the animal, it would instantly go for the fresh and bloody stuff but for some reason when our humans are in charge we tend to turn our noses up at it that raw.

She snatches it out of my grasp and I grin as I drop the second by her paws, knowing she'll easily eat two. Her tiger should be out hunting but, even though she's safe in our territory with the extra patrols we've put on and having the extra people around, she's still too fragile and struggling to trust that safety. And to be honest, I don't really blame her not after all she's been through.

I watch as she swipes at her whiskers with paws before commencing to clean them, seeming content with her midnight snack. "I'm going to see what I can find to watch on the TV. Come and join me when you're done cleaning yourself up," I suggest, aware that she'll need time for her food to settle and a quick run in the yard before she's ready to curl back up for more sleep.

As I open the lounge door the quiet sound of voices reaches my ears and I spot the flickering of the TV screen.

Ruby's head pops up over the back of the sofa. "Did I wake you? Your mum insisted the TV wouldn't disturb anyone."

I shake my head as I pull the door to, making sure to leave it ajar enough for Little Tiger to get her paw or snout in when she's ready to join us. "You didn't, I didn't even know you were here until I opened the door. All the rooms are soundproofed. So as long as the door's shut no one will hear a thing from in here."

She glances over my shoulder at the partially opened door, a wary look on her face.

"We've got someone in animal form joining us in a minute. It's okay though, everyone sleeps with the bedroom doors shut so nothing will get through to them."

Accepting my assurance she turns back to the TV and I sit in the other corner of the three-seater sofa. "What are you watching?"

"You'll laugh."

"I promise I won't." I draw a cross over my heart to reiterate my point.

"Fine… It's a teen movie called '*To all the Boys I've Loved Before*'."

I smile, but manage to hold back my laugh. I made a promise after all. "You're showing your age, Rubes."

Ruby leans over the empty space between us to slap my bicep. "Piss off. I knew I should have switched it off the second you sat down."

I rub at my arm then reach out to stop her from turning it off. "I'm only kidding. It's got nothing to do with age.

People of all ages watch those teen movies. Bel loves those kinds of movies."

She rolls her eyes. "Who do you think recommended I watch it?"

I nod, feeling a little dumb. "I should have known."

The door clicks and we both watch as Little Tiger steps around the corner of the sofa before sitting by my feet. She gives Ruby a narrow stare.

Ruby's eyes widen for a second before she plasters on a friendly smile. "Are you going to introduce us then, Jared?"

Sitting forward in my seat I drop my hand to Little Tiger's head as she nudges my leg obviously wanting the introduction too. "Little Tiger."

She snaps at my fingers and I let out a laugh.

"I keep telling you, all you have to do is shift and tell us your real name and I won't call you it anymore." I shake my head as she lets out a huff. I think she likes it really and just pretends she doesn't, seeing her so playful warms my heart.

"Anyway...Little Tiger, this is my friend Ruby." I nod towards Ruby. "Ruby, this is Little Tiger..." I pause as I mull over the rest of the sentence floating around in my head. *Pride.* Feeling it with my whole being I carry on. "The newest member of my pride."

Little Tiger's eyes are soft and glowing with gratitude.

"Well then," Ruby starts, catching Little Tiger's attention, her eyes flicking from me to her in an instant.

I swallow a lump in my throat as something shifts within the pride bonds, causing all kinds of emotions to overwhelm me. The fact that she's accepted me as her alpha so easily and quickly tells me she knows she'll never find her family. Although I'm so happy about her acceptance, I'm also heartbroken over that fact because that means she must have seen their deaths to know that they aren't out there looking for her. No kid should have to see things like that.

"Since you don't like the name Jared is calling you, how would you feel about me calling you Tiggy?"

Little Tiger tilts her head to the side, obviously giving the name some thought, before she jumps to her feet and licks at Ruby's knee.

"Tiggy it is," Ruby states with a giggle.

Little Tiger turns to me a confused glint in her eyes. I was wondering how long it would take for her to notice Ruby was…different.

"Ruby isn't a shifter, she's a vampire."

Little Tiger's energy changes in a split second. Her hackles rise and she releases a threatening hiss. I can only guess she's had a bad experience with a vampire in the past.

"I don't know who you've met of my kind but I promise you I will never hurt you. I only take blood that is willingly given."

Little Tiger seems to weigh up Ruby for a few seconds before relaxing her stance and jumping on the sofa between us. She circles a time or two and finally settles down curled around her tail.

"Tiggy," Ruby pauses until Little Tiger lifts her head and she knows she's listening. "You need to know I'm not the only vampire here. My sire is here too." Ruby must see something in Little Tiger's eyes because she hurries her next words. "He won't hurt you either."

Feeling her anxiety through the pride bonds I can tell she wants to believe what Ruby is saying but she's obviously struggling to trust her. Reaching out, I run my hand over her back allowing her to feel my alpha energy. "You're safe," I repeat my words hoping to drill the statement into her so that one day she won't doubt it.

After thirty minutes of watching the teen movie Little Tiger jumps off the sofa and gives me a look that says *'what are you waiting for?'*

I smirk. "I guess that's my cue to leave." Standing, I stretch my arms over my head and groan as my joints crack.

"Your age is showing, Jared," Ruby teases.

The door opens and I turn to spot Dominick waltzing in, his hair looking dishevelled and his clothes clearly thrown on without much thought. "What are you going to torture me with tonight, Ruby? Oooh…a party."

"Sadly not. We were just leaving," I say as I make my way towards the door only to have Little Tiger wrap herself around my legs causing me to stumble; my lion's reflexes being the only thing keeping me upright.

"Tiggy, this is the other vampire I told you about, Dominick, my sire." Little Tiger stays close to my side but doesn't make herself a tripping hazard anymore so I once again make my way to the door. Dominick stays quiet, which I know is a mean feat for him, so clearly he can sense the tiger cub's wariness of him.

"Do you want to go straight to bed, or do you need a quick run around the yard first?" I ask as I pull the door closed behind us.

She shakes out her fur and pounces up the stairs in answer and I follow, looking forward to nothing more than getting a few hours of sleep curled around my mate's warm body.

20

IT'S WAR

I LOOK out at the warehouse from behind the bushes, Jared's energy playing over my skin like an electric pulse as he crouches beside me.

"Are you ready?" Jared asks as we watch Misty chant out another spell, her mates on either side of her just outside the line of trees and bushes.

We'd originally planned on Misty pulling down the Cleaners' wards but she'd said the second they go down they'll know we're here—and that would ruin the element of surprise that we're hoping for—so instead Misty is putting up her own wards which should help cloak us from detection.

"Ready to show them they messed with the wrong people." My voice is laced with anger, an anger that I'm sure every one of us here today shares.

Misty gives a nod towards Theo—who is crouched in the bush a few metres to the left of Jared and I. Dominick whisks Misty away in that special popping way of his and within seconds he's back standing beside his mate, Billy, who is already shifting into his wolf form.

On his return Theo lets out a whistle—the signal to shift, for those who are planning to fight in animal form. I grimace at the loud shrill unable to understand Theo's trust in something he can't see—if Misty's wards haven't worked they'll know we're here.

"You okay?" Jared asks, obviously noticing my unease, perhaps even sensing it through our bond.

I nod before taking a second to stretch my neck out trying to ease the tension. "Yeah. I'll just be glad when we're home and safe again."

I've seen what these psychos can do and the kind of weapons they have to play with. I'd have to be an idiot not to be worried. It's extremely unlikely we'll all make it home unscathed, even with the element of surprise.

Jared reaches out and rubs at my shoulders, helping me relax. "Just look after yourself in there. And let everyone else worry about themselves." I give a small nod, clearly not convincing enough because Jared goes on. "Sass, everyone here is a strong fighter, trust that they can handle this."

Theo lets out a wolf whistle and within seconds we're all charging for the building. I'm prepared for the overwhelming sounds after stepping through their wards, but I notice the other guys' steps falter, even though they'd been warned. Not like I blame them, it's one of the most disorientating things I've ever experienced.

We're soon storming through the doors and windows, following the plan of mass entry. As we step into the warehouse and find no sign of counterattack it's confirmed that Misty's wards have held up. It's not like you can break windows and knock down doors without making a noise.

A handful of us break off and head to where the prisoners are being kept while everyone else charges towards the complex's dining and sleeping quarters.

Jared and I lead the way into the prison section and as soon as we round the corner a guard jumps up from the seat he'd been lazing in, his eyes wide with surprise.

The guard raises the rifle hanging at his side, pointing it at the wolf beside me, but before he can get a shot off Jared is pushing the gun into the air. Fear permeates the air and the animals in the cages go wild throwing themselves against the bars.

Jared holds the guy by his throat, the gun discarded across the floor. I have a clear view of his profile and watch as he stares at the guard intently. "I guess you did a lot of nasty things to them." The guard gives him nothing but a stony-faced look and Jared flicks his eyes to me. "Let them out. They deserve to have this kill."

"They deserve to have a lot of kills," I mutter as I step up to the first cage, which contains a tan coloured wolf. My hands burn as I tug at the padlock on the cage, making me aware that it's made with silver. It snaps with ease—thanks to my supernatural strength and anger—and as soon as the door creaks open the wolf pushes out and pounces on the guard. Something eases inside me at the sound of his piercing screams; at least justice is finally being done.

Another wolf joins the first along with a kangaroo, and I look around to see Harriet from the Falls Creek Pack and Gareth from the Rossi Pack both unlocking cages. I move onto another and another until all the shifters are free.

I take in the sight of the room and it's obvious by the bloody mess left where I'd last seen the guard that he's dead. A clattering sound catches my attention and I follow the noise to a storeroom, the room I'd discovered to be the artillery when we'd been on our recon mission.

I find Jared with a gun in hand and a pile of them at his feet, all bent out of shape. The sound of footsteps comes towards us and I spin to find five people charging into the doorway I'd just come through; their eyes wide as they take in the destruction of the weapons before them. Weapons they'd clearly come to collect and use on our people.

Two of them run at me and the remaining three go for Jared, obviously thinking he's the bigger threat—and rightly so. He is an alpha after all.

Not giving them a chance to get the upper hand I kick out at the guy who's closest to me. My foot connects with his knee. The snapping sound and the scream he releases as he collapses tells me I hit my mark and incapacitated him.

A fist connects with my cheekbone, the female having caught me while distracted over the guy, and I finally turn my attention to her. I block another punch with my left arm as I hit out with my right and manage to get a solid punch at her neck. She coughs and splutters as she clutches at her throat, and I know I've done some serious damage.

A strand of hair falls across my face and I blow it away as I spin to find Jared with his opponents dead at his feet. Seeing he's got everything in hand, I pull the spare hair tie I always wear on my wrist off and quickly scrape my hair back, making sure to get it all back even those pesky shorter strands at the front too.

Jared strides towards the guy who is still rolling on the floor cradling his knee. Lifting his foot he kicks the guy in the face with so much force his neck cracks.

I stare at him with wide eyes, disbelieving that he'd just ended someone who was already down and incapacitated.

"They don't deserve to be given mercy. Not after all they've done," Jared states, his golden eyes bore into me as he passes making it clear his lion's in the forefront. I nod in agreement, after all he's right. Although now I'm left thinking they deserve worse than the quick death he just gave them.

I BRUSH my fingers over my mate's arm as we leave the armoury hoping to ease the sting of my harsh tone. With my lion so close to the surface I'm finding it hard to keep his anger at bay. Vengeance is all he can focus on.

"You're right." She gives me a sly smile. "Let's go give them all what they deserve."

We follow the sound of grunts and flesh impacting flesh as we head back through the warehouse towards the living quarters. It's complete chaos. Fists are flying, bodies are falling to the ground, and the sounds of gunshots are ringing through the air. We're hardly even in the sectioned off space and Saskia jumps into the fray.

Seeing three guys fighting Theo, I decide to even the odds by jumping in. I throw a punch, hitting one guy on the jaw. He's a big guy and barely acknowledges the hit as he whips out a fist in my direction.

I duck but not before the knuckle duster scratches across my cheekbone, the burning sting it leaves behind telling me that it's made of silver.

"Fucker."

Theo chuckles beside me as he fights, knocking out one of his two remaining opponents. "By the way, he's wearing silver knuckle dusters."

"Yeah. Thanks for that. I'd never have guessed." I roll my

eyes as I kick my leg at the big guy, my enhanced speed surprising him and easily taking his legs from under him.

"Freaks," he grumbles as he gets to his feet.

Theo's remaining opponent falls and he turns to face the big guy. Making it two against one, not that we'd need it. I'd only been playing with him anyway. Humans have no chance against us when it comes to one on one combat. Our strength and speed are just too much for them.

The only chance they have is with weapons and the fact that I can't hear any more gunshots makes me think their guns have all been taken out.

"*Death to all!*" A voice calls out.

Panic flickers in my opponent's eyes before he pulls open his shirt to reveal what looks like a suicide vest. My heart races in my chest at the sight, as the need to protect my mate surges through me. Forgetting the guy in front of me I search the space for Saskia.

"BOMB!" I hear Theo shout as I charge across the room.

Saskia turns at his words and our eyes connect as I leap into the air. My bones crack and realign as my skin turns to fur. My body shifting to lion form seconds before I make contact with Saskia, knocking her to the ground. The flesh on my back burns as shrapnel hits me, and my body is overwhelmed with pain, but relief washes through me knowing I've protected my mate—managing to cover her from head to foot with my heavy form just in time.

22

PANIC AND TERROR

SASKIA

MY EARS ARE RINGING in time with the throbbing pain on the crown of my head. Jared had knocked me off my feet so quickly I hadn't even had a chance to brace for a fall, so my head had hit the concrete floor pretty hard.

I shove at Jared, not sure what part of him I'm connecting with but hoping to shift him off me. He doesn't budge an inch, his unconscious form like a dead weight.

"Jared," I call out in the hope that my voice will bring him back to consciousness. I cough as I inhale a mouth full of dust.

Cracking my eyes open hesitantly, in case of a concussion, I peak out into the darkness. I can't see much but a cloud of dust from the angle my head is at. Thankfully Jared didn't land on my face or I'd be suffocating under his fur.

That thought swirls through my head and my fingers search for his fur. My movements becoming panicked as my heart races in my chest. It's his human flesh that I can feel beneath my fingertips, not fur. Knowing he was in lion form when he landed has terror flowing through me. Even though he's unconscious he should still be lion, there was no time or reason for him to shift back to human. Knowing our bodies shift back to human when we die in our animal form I scream out for help.

"*Help!*" I feel tears roll out the corners of my eyes as I fear the worst. "Someone, please…Help."

I hear a scuffling noise beside my head. "Sassy?" Matty calls out.

"Here. It's Jared. I think he—" My words cut off. He can't be. My lioness's panic washes over me taking my breath away.

Mate.

Mate.

MATE. The word repeats in my head getting louder and more frantic sounding each time. Yet my panic subsides because with that one word I know Jared isn't dead, because if he were I'd feel it through our bond. I reach inside myself and feel him, he's weak and in pain but he's alive.

His weight lifts off me and I scramble to get up, not caring who had lifted him off me, so that I can see him and whatever injuries he has.

"*Jared!*" Grigori's voice booms through the warehouse and I suddenly realise my ears have healed themselves and are no longer ringing.

"He's alive," I say, even though I know he'll be able to feel as much through the pride bonds. Hell, he'd probably used them to feel him way before I thought of it.

I try to push Jared on his back so I can see his face but the person holding him keeps him steady, his nose centimetres from the floor.

"No!" I look up to find Theo's emerald green eyes shining with concern. "He's got silver shards in his back."

My eyes widen and I shift my position so I can see for myself. "Oh, Jar." No wonder he's unconscious and so gravely ill. His back, bum and legs are speckled with sharp little pieces of silver. He looks like a pincushion.

I don't waste any time in picking them out, not caring that my fingertips are blistering up at the contact with the silver. Anger courses through me and I can't stop myself from berating him whilst my fingers work. "Why didn't you run the other way, for fuck's sake?"

Grigori appears at my side his fingers joining mine in the daunting task before us.

"My life is not worth more than yours." A tear trails down my cheek but I ignore it, not caring that others are watching me.

Another set of hands join us and I look up to find the Vampire King eyes intent on his fingers moving at a supernatural speed over Jared's legs.

"That's all that we're going to get out," Dominick states.

As much as I know it's the truth, I don't want to admit it. My eyes fall on Grigori. "What about drawing it out, like we did with the others."

Grigori looks torn, but he shakes his head nevertheless. "It's too dangerous. You nearly died." He gives me a grim look. "I can't have your death on my hands even if it saves my son."

"I'm stronger now. I'm his mate." I reach out to try but Matty pulls me away at the nod of Grigori. I twist and turn trying to get free but his hold only tightens.

"Don't fight me, Saskia. Please." His voice is full of torment but I don't care I need to try everything I can to save my mate.

My lioness roars inside me.

She wants me to let her out.

Seeing no chance of getting free from Matty like this, I let her come forward and set her free.

With the crack of my first bones breaking Matty releases me and takes a step back. A clever move when you think about it. It's not like he'd want a sharp claw to catch any of his soft vulnerable flesh and tear it apart in seconds.

Before the tingles even start to leave, my lioness takes us over to our mate. Settling down beside him, a whimper escapes our snout. His pain comes through so much stronger in my animal form. She pulls back slightly allowing me into the forefront, giving me the ability to control our movements once again.

Resting my head over Jared's back, I close my eyes as I feel it rise and fall with his laboured breaths. Highly aware that I need to do something to help him I draw on my energy and our mate bond, wishing with all my being that I could draw out those tiny pieces of silver that are slowly poisoning him to death.

I hear a gasp but don't let it distract me.

"Fuck!" Grigori curses as I feel him drop beside me.

His energy ripples against my fur and I know without even looking that he's joined me in trying to draw the silver out. Two more alpha energies swirl around us making it obvious that Jesse and Theo have stepped in to help too.

Jared's breathing evens out and my heart finally leaves my throat, settling back where it belongs. My energy seems to deplete along with it and I feel my body change shape as my mind starts to drift away. The only thought floating around it is the fact that my mate is no longer on the cusp of death.

23

PAINFUL SHIFT

JARED

IT'S BEEN two days since we descended upon The Cleaners' warehouse. With the help of her mates and a bit of magic, Misty had managed to draw the silver from those who had been too close to the bombs when they'd gone off. The big guy I'd been fighting wasn't the only one wearing a suicide vest. It seems like our strike hadn't been a complete surprise to them after all.

The shifters that had been held captive are somehow stuck in their animal forms, which explains why Little Tiger hasn't shifted since we found her. Misty thinks it's a spell from the Cleaners' mage or witch but that would also mean they weren't at the warehouse when the bombs went off. If they'd been killed the spell would be broken—and we know all the Cleaners that were in the warehouse are deceased.

I think regardless of whether everyone in the Cleaners' cell was there that night or not, they won't rush back into attacking shifters around here. They'd need time to regroup and make new plans, learning from any mistakes they made with us. Hopefully they'll move on and find another town to attack. One they think is unsuspecting. *We'll ensure that won't happen.*

Jesse, the Rossi Pack Alpha, set up an online communication portal for shifters who want to stay connected when he lost his mate. He's going to extend it to all supernatural creatures with the help of Dominick, the Mount Roxby Vampire

King, and utilise it to spread a word of warning about the Cleaners and their actions.

Saskia sighs beside me and my heart leaps in my chest. She's been comatose since the warehouse and, although I know she's just in a deep healing sleep—I can feel it through the bonds after all—I just can't seem to stop myself from worrying. She'd been so stupid to deplete all her energy saving me like that.

Her arm stretches out, searching over the bed sheets. When it comes into contact with my abs she shuffles over until she's burying her face against my chest.

"Hey…"

"Hey?" I let out an unamused laugh. "That's all I get. You almost killed yourself to heal me and all you have is *'hey'*?"

Her fingers trail over my abs as she presses gentle butterfly kisses over my heart. "You risked your life for mine first, so don't pull the putting yourself in danger card with me."

"But Sass, I risked my life because I needed to protect you. Then you put yourself in danger when I wasn't alert enough to stop you." That's what tortured me the most, if she'd died when I'd been too weak to help…I couldn't even bear to think about that outcome.

She tilts her head and pins me with a demanding stare. "You knew who I was before you claimed me as your mate. If you wanted a princess you wouldn't have chosen me."

I tug her up my body needing to have her closer, needing to taste her. "That doesn't mean I'm not terrified."

"Well, how about we both agree to not put ourselves in danger? That way we won't need to protect each other," she offers, her eyes glued to my lips as her tongue pokes out to lick at her own.

"Deal." I seal it with a hard demanding kiss, all the while

knowing as hard as either of us try; our deal is impossible to stick to. A shifter's life is dangerous and our need to protect the other will always come first over our safety. That's just how we're wired.

The doorbell on my bedroom door chimes and Saskia breaks the kiss with a groan. "Seriously? We can't have two minutes?"

"Two minutes? I'd need more than two minutes, Sass." I pull the covers over Saskia's back to ensure she's not on display and hold her against me as I push the button on the bedside table that unlocks the soundproof door.

The door opens and Theo comes into view.

"This better be important." I state.

"Ha! How the tables have turned," Theo says, highly amused. I'd cock blocked him a number of times lately so I guess he should be allowed to enjoy his moment. He doesn't enjoy it long, his face suddenly turning serious. "Misty thinks she has the spell to free the others from their animal forms worked out. We figured you'd want to be there for Little Tiger."

I nod. "Thanks. We'll be down in a few minutes."

Theo turns and pulls the door to but just before it closes all the way he pokes his head back in. "It's good to see you awake at last, Saskia. Your mate was a nightmare to be around while he waited for you to surface." He disappears just as quickly as he reappeared and Sassy turns her face to mine.

"How long was I out?"

"Two days."

"And you were a nightmare to be around?" She gives me a raised brow, clearly thinking I didn't have a right to act in such a way.

"It was the longest two days of my life."

She laughs, and I quickly silence her, crushing my lips against hers in a demanding kiss.

———

DAD GREATS Saskia with a gentle hug as we step into the moonlit backyard. "It's a relief to have you back, sweetheart."

Saskia eyes him warily. "Was he really that bad?"

Dad looks to me and back to her before nodding. "Yes."

I roll my eyes. "Thanks Dad."

"Well, if this oaf didn't throw himself in front of a bomb I wouldn't have needed to drain my own energy."

I open my mouth to argue but Dad beats me to it.

"If he hadn't have jumped in front of you, you'd be dead and he would have been…" He shakes his head. "It doesn't bear thinking about."

I tug at Saskia's hips, turning her to face me. "He's right," I state before pressing a quick kiss against her lips and throwing an arm over her shoulder. "Let's get these people freely shifting."

The backyard is, thankfully, pretty big, so it easily fits the dozen prisoners we'd freed from the warehouse along with the alphas from the guest packs and a couple of betas and enforcers.

Misty clears her throat. "Hi." She flicks her eyes over the alphas and betas. "I think the best way to do this is as a group spell; everyone all at once. But that's going to take a lot of energy and that's why I've asked you all here."

I glance around and although I see a few frowns I can tell that they are only out of curiosity and nothing else.

"If you are willing to help I'll ask you to make a circle around those affected and join hands. I'll then draw on your energies to counteract the spell. This will only work if you are willing to share your energy. If you don't think that's something you can do, then feel free to walk away, no hard feelings."

People start to shift around but they don't leave, instead within seconds a circle is formed, hands are held, and we all look to Misty for guidance.

"Thank you. I'm sure they'll all appreciate your assistance, and I most definitely do."

Billy nods. "I do too. This is taxing on my mate so the fact that so many of you are willing to help her eases my mind somewhat."

Billy's words have me wondering whether Saskia should be part of the circle. She's just woken up from a deep healing coma after depleting her energy for me.

She catches me watching her and lets out a sigh. "I'll be okay. I promise."

I watch her for a few more seconds and decide I have to trust her and respect her decision. She's strong and determined; most definitely not a mate that can be wrapped in cotton wool. I give her hand a gentle squeeze, hopefully conveying that I'll take her word and not fight her on it.

Misty starts to chant words I don't recognise and I focus all my energy through the hands I'm holding. She chants the same five-word phrase over and over. Her words becoming louder, faster, and more frantic with each time.

The animals in the middle of the circle are watching Misty intently, clearly not feeling any effects of the spell she's trying to cast.

Just as I start to think it's not going to work, the wolf closest to Misty howls as it drops to the floor, its body contorting as each bone breaks and realigns. As his fur seemingly melts off, revealing tanned skin, the kangaroo beside him lets out a whimper.

One by one each of the animals shift into their human

forms. The pink puckered scars that cover their bodies have me seething with anger. I bite back a roar but I can't seem to stop the fury that flicks out from my energy. Little Tiger steps out from the crowd and stops in front of me fear in her eyes. I make a move to comfort her but Saskia and Billy hold tight to my hands.

"You can't break the circle," Billy states, leaving me so conflicted about what to do.

I kneel so that I'm eye to eye with her, all the while keeping the circle whole. "Sweetheart. I'm sorry if I scared you. I'm just mad that they hurt you all like they did."

She licks at my cheek and as her body starts to shake and more whimpers escape from her snout, I know the shift is upon her.

"Don't fight, Little Tiger. Let it flow through you." I push all of my alpha energy through the circle as I try to talk her through the shift, hoping my calming tone will allow her to do as I say and ease the pain, even if it's just a little.

Her eyes stay glued to mine the whole way through her change and in a matter of minutes I'm faced with a beautiful little girl who could be no older than ten.

My eyes instantly drop to the angry wound on her neck that I know goes the whole way around. A wound that will stay with her forever in the form of a nasty scar, and a reminder of things that no child should go through.

Across the circle, Ruby ducks under her mate's, Eddie, and Theo's joined hands, a bundle of clothes in her arms. She passes garments to people as she walks by, her eyes never leaving the small figure in front of me.

"Hey Tiggy, wrap this around you." Showing she knows shifters well she's careful not to touch Little Tiger's sensitive skin as she holds out the zip up hoodie.

"T—" Little Tiger clears her throat and tries to talk

again. "Thanks." She takes the hoodie and wraps it around herself. It buries her and I belatedly realise it's one of mine.

I give Ruby a grateful smile. It was smart giving her something covered in a scent she feels safe with. Her emotions will be all over the place, having been stuck in her animal form for god only knows how long, and she'll appreciate the comfort my scent will give her.

24

UNEXPECTED ARRIVAL

I WATCH in admiration as Jared fusses over Little Tiger—who we now know is called Mazikeen, or Maze for short—making sure she feels comfortable and safe. Being in her human form will make her animal feel vulnerable. He'd been amazing with her whilst she was in her animal form so I shouldn't be surprised by the attention he's been giving her since she shifted last night. He's a born alpha with compassion pouring off him.

It turns out The Cleaners had her for months. They'd executed her father and taken her, along with her older sister and mother. Unfortunately, she's the only one that survived the torture. Perhaps with her being younger they weren't as brutal with her, or maybe she was just lucky.

The story is similar with each of the survivors. They were picked up in groups and very few of them managed to stay together. Some insist that their family member had been taken to another camp or sold off as a plaything because they'd feel their deaths through their bonds and they haven't. Others just feel that those people are in denial and a bond is easy enough to mute if you don't want the loved ones you are connected to to feel the terrible things you might be going through. Whatever it may be, we can only go on what we're told and what we saw at the warehouse. Either ending could be the reality. And I personally don't know which one would be the best.

"Are you ready to join the party?"

Maze gives Jared a wary look as she bites at her bottom lip. After a moments hesitation she straightens her shoulders and gives him a nod. "Yes."

A pop sound, that's strangely becoming familiar to me has me spinning around, but instead of finding Ruby or Dominick before me I find myself faced with someone I hadn't ever expected to see in Quilpie again.

"Rosabel."

"Saskia." Her tone is full of animosity and I don't exactly blame her. I wasn't one that was openly against her but I never really made life easy for her either. "I didn't mean to startle you. I wasn't expecting anyone to be in here. I thought everyone would be outside enjoying the party."

I wave her off. "You're fine. What with Dominick and Ruby we're getting used to people popping in and out."

"Hey Bel," Jared starts, a frown creasing his brow. "I didn't know you were coming."

"I invited her," Grigori states from the open doorway leading into the kitchen. "I felt it was the best time to let the pride put the past behind them."

Upon seeing Rosabel, I'd initially been concerned but hearing Grigori's words I couldn't agree more.

"It's good to see you again, Bel. Your aunt and uncle are going to be thrilled to see you." Grigori disappears back through the kitchen as quickly as he appears not giving Bel a chance to reply to his greeting.

Jared steps forward and pulls her into a hug. I can't stop myself from fisting my hands at my sides, knowing it's the knowledge of their previous relationship causing it.

A gentle hand clamps down on my shoulder. "They're family, nothing else." Theo's words settle my lioness quicker than the human side of me. But knowing what he says is the truth, I relax my hands and take a deep calming breath, pushing away the jealousy raging through me.

Bel releases Jared and comes towards us. I step back expecting her to wrap her open arms around her mate, so I stumble in surprise when she envelopes me in a friendly hug.

"I'm so glad someone finally managed to capture his lion. He deserves to feel the love of a mate."

I give her a stunned look as she releases me. I didn't expect her to be so happy he'd mated with someone from the pride. Thankfully she doesn't seem to expect a reply from me as she throws herself at her mate because she's left me speechless.

"You missed me," Theo says, his tone almost like a purr. Making it clear where his head's at and we probably shouldn't stick around.

"Okay Maze, I think we should join the party now," I quickly suggest.

Jared scoops Maze up and throws her over his shoulder. "That is a very good idea."

Maze's exuberant giggles are music to my ears and I find myself grinning along with her as I follow Jared through the house.

Excitement fills me as I take in the happy laughter that fills the street. Grigori has done an amazing job of organising the street party. People have been running around all day, lining the street with tables and chairs.

A handful of barbecues are set up at one end and there is even a bouncy castle for the kids at the other. There are some giant games scattered down the street—Jenga, Dominoes and Chess. It's the balloons and bunting tied to fences and streetlights that tie it all together.

Matty throws me a wave from behind a table set up as a DJ stand and I give him an animated one back. A classic hit sounds through the speakers and some of the older generation whoop and cheer, clearly happy with Matty's song choice. It makes me grin because I know how much it'll be killing him to not play his hip-hop favourites.

As the song ends Grigori's voice booms through the speakers, the partygoers excited voices immediately hush, and I give Jared a questioning glance wondering if he knows anything about his father's announcement. He gives me a quick shake of his head before focusing on Grigori and the microphone in his hand.

"Don't worry, I don't plan on disrupting the party for too long. I just wanted to inform those that no longer have a pack, pride or whatever group you belong to, you are more than welcome to settle here and join our pride."

There are a few mumbled remarks that although I can't exactly make them out, it's clear it isn't anything nice but Grigori ignores them and forges on. "I think with recent events the pride can see that we are not enemies. We are all shifters. And even with the help of Misty, Dominick and Ruby, we can stretch that to supernatural creatures. We need to be there for each other as allies and friends. So, anyone that needs a home is welcome in my pride."

"My pack feels the same," Theo calls out.

"As does mine," Jesse states.

Ryan catches attention by holding up his hand. "My alpha offers the same of our pack."

"Now that's sorted, let's enjoy the evening," Grigori states before handing the mic back to Matty who, with a click of a couple of switches, quickly has some beating rhythm pumping through the speakers.

————

JARED'S ENERGY encircles me seconds before his arms slide around my waist. "Here's my Sassy Girl." His lips press a kiss against the curve of my shoulder, the warmth of his breath sending shivers down my spine. "I feel like you've been hiding from me all day."

Needing to face him, I turn in his arms. "I haven't been hiding. You've been busy." My tone comes out a little angrier than I'd anticipated so I press a kiss to his lips, hoping to ease the sting and show him I'm not as upset as I sounded.

The world around us seems to fall away as we sway in time with the slow tune playing out of Matty's speakers.

The song soon changes, breaking the romantic moment. I find myself watching the people around us and suddenly realise life as I know it will have to change.

"Are we going to travel back to Mount Roxby with the others?" I ask, bringing my thoughts out in the open.

"*We?*"

I watch as he flinches, no doubt at the eagerness in his own voice.

He may want to breakaway from the pride and I know he'll be willing to stick around for me—*his mate*—but there's no way I'm forcing him to do that.

I use my hands to grab his hair and tug his head towards mine so we're eye to eye. I need him to see that I mean every word I say. "Mount Roxby has become your home. You have a pride and family there." His eyes rise and I know he has questions but I carry on. "Family isn't always by blood. You can choose family too, and the people I've seen you with from Mount Roxby are just that; your chosen family. I could never expect you to walk away from that."

The look in his eyes softens and he crushes his lips against mine in a passionate kiss.

I moan into his mouth, thinking I'll never get enough of his kisses even if he gives me a thousand. I pull back and open my eyes, the twinkling lights behind Jared's head make it feel like we're somewhere magical and not in the middle of Main Street.

"You're so beautiful. How did I get so lucky to be able to call you my mate?"

Sliding my hands out of his hair I lock them around the back of his neck and look up at him in wonder. "I think I'm the lucky one."

Jared presses his mouth against mine in a desperate kiss as his hands hold me against him. He breaks the kiss too soon for my liking and I whimper in complaint. He lets out a chuckle and presses his lips to my forehead. "I won't leave you hanging. I promise."

Removing one hand from my back and he pulls his phone from his back pocket. I make a move to step back and give him room but he holds me tight with his other hand and after a few taps at the screen with his thumb, he slips his phone away and scoops me up into his arms.

I let out a squeal of surprise, feeling my face heat as I spot people looking our way.

Jared strides away from the party with sure steps that tell me he has a destination in mind and, as he turns into his parents' yard, my body buzzes with anticipation.

I know exactly where he's heading and I can more than imagine all that he has in mind to do there.

25

EASE AT LAST

JARED

I STARE DOWN in awe at the sight of Saskia laid out naked on my bed. I wasn't just saying it when I'd told Sass that I didn't know how I'd managed to get so lucky to call her my mate. I meant it with every fibre of my being. It's a feeling I don't think I'll ever lose.

"Are you going to stop gawping and get naked or should I get dressed and head back to the party?" Saskia's cheeky question matches her playful grin.

I pull off my clothes one by one and I feel my own lips rise into a smile as she watches eagerly, the scent of her arousal filling the air.

Once I've removed my last piece of clothing I crawl onto the bed and kiss my way up Saskia's body. Forcing myself to take each inch torturously slow. As I reach the apex of her thighs Saskia squirms beneath me, clearly trying to get my attention on the parts craving my touch. I'm not ready to cut things short just yet so I skip up her body and press my lips against the softness of her stomach.

"That's not fair. Go back down," she complains.

Lifting my head, I give her a mischievous smile. "What? To here?" I drop my mouth against her inner thigh, just above the knee, and give it a lap of my tongue before peppering kisses over her knee and down her calf.

She releases a growl and I can't help but laugh. "You know exactly where I mean."

Skipping my lips over to the other leg, I kiss my way up her calf and over the knee until I feel like it has received the same amount of attention as the first leg. Only then do I lick and kiss my way higher to where we both know she needs it.

I tease her clit with my tongue and in no time she's purring beneath me. I smile at the sound, knowing she's enjoying what I'm doing to her. I slide my tongue lower and slip it into her, savouring her taste and warm embrace.

"Jar…" My name is like a whispered prayer off her lips, the sound turning me on and making my semi hard dick become steel in an instant.

Moving my tongue back to her clit I use my fingers to check she's ready for me. Inserting one at first, followed by a second. When I feel her body shake beneath me I know she's close to orgasm. I gently bite down on her clit and it pulls her over the edge just as I'd wanted.

I kiss my way up her body as she comes back down, pausing at each pebbled nipple to give them a moment of attention.

Saskia's hands grip at my biceps as she tries to lift me higher up. I go willingly, needing to be one with her. Her mouth crushes against mine as soon as I'm in reach.

The kiss isn't pretty, all teeth, tongues and need.

My cock pulsates between us and Sass breaks the kiss.

"I need my mate." Her eyes flash to her lioness's, making it clear they are both close to the surface.

"He's all yours, Sassy Girl." Lifting my body, I position myself against her entrance grateful that I don't need to make her wait while I suit up. Shifters only have chance of pregnancy when the female is in heat and I can sense that Saskia isn't right now. We also can't catch sexually trans-mitted diseases so there is no need to use protection. I inch my way in torturously slow.

Saskia bites her bottom lip and releases a moan of pleasure, as I slowly inch my way in. "You feel…"

"So good," I finish, when she trails off.

"Mmm." Her eyes close and the room fills with our mating scent.

A scent that spurs me on to take her hard and fast, how I know she likes it.

———

HAVING LEFT Saskia in the shower—if I'd have stayed any longer I'd have gotten carried away and we'd never have gotten down for breakfast, I walk into the open plan kitchen and dining room to find it full to the brim with my chosen family.

Theo, Eddie, and Little Tiger are all sitting at the dining table chatting to my dad, while Misty and Billy are helping my mum cook. The only people missing are the two vampires, and rightly so, since they're stuck in their slumber until sunset.

Having been so focused on Alyssa and her recovery lately I've not really had the chance to see Misty, Billy and Dominick together. When I'd first heard about them I didn't believe it. Billy had always seemed to be all for the women but having seen the three of them together while they've been here I couldn't see them working any other way.

"Are you coming back with us? There's space on the bus," Theo asks when he spots me across the room.

I give Mum a kiss in the cheek as I pass and she hands me a mug of coffee. "No, Saskia has things to sort out, and she'll need her car in Mount Roxby anyway, so we'll head down in a day or two," I state as I take a seat beside my dad.

"Good answer. Your mum would be a nightmare to live with if you ran off without spending at least a day with her."

Dad grinned next to me but I knew every word he'd said was the truth. Not only would she be a nightmare for him to live with but she'd probably never forgive me either.

"Too right!" Mum calls across the kitchen, making it clear she was listening to our conversation even whilst cooking and chatting with the others.

Dad eyes me warily. "Is your mate happy about the move?"

"It was her idea."

His eyes widen at my admission. "You would have stayed in Quilpie if she hadn't suggested the move?"

I shrug. "I wouldn't have left without her."

Gentle hands slide over my shoulders as Saskia's energy surrounds me and her scent fills the air. "And I would never have made you choose between me and the place that's become your home."

"Aww… Listen to that. My baby found himself a mate and a good one at that." My face flames at Mum's comments.

Saskia giggles against my cheek as she presses her lips there. "Did you hear that, Babe? A good one…" She steps to my side and pulls out the empty seat beside me.

Twisting in my chair, I pull Saskia onto my lap, causing her to release a squeal. "I didn't just hear. I know." I plant a sloppy kiss on her lips and the kitchen erupts into catcalls thanks to Eddie and Theo, the childish bastards. If it were their mates here they'd be all over them. We break apart and I flip the guys across the table the bird.

Little Tiger giggles and Saskia slaps me on the shoulder. "There are kids present."

"Yeah. How could you be so irresponsible, Jared? Some alpha you are," Eddie teases.

Little Tiger's smile drops, and a frown creases her brow. "He's a good alpha," she states, her tone making it clear there is no room for argument, and the anger pulsing off her telling us how serious she is.

Eddie's face falls. "Oh sweetie, I was only joking. I promise." Reaching out he places his hand over hers and gives it a gentle squeeze. "He's one of the best alpha's out there."

"Of course he is, he learnt everything he knows from my husband," Mum states, giving Dad an admiring look as she places a plate teaming with a cooked breakfast in front of him.

Billy and Misty join us at the table, handing out plates as they pass.

"Let's eat," Billy says as he sits down beside his mate. "We need to get on the road. We have a long trip ahead of us."

Placing my knife and fork on the empty plate, I sit back in my seat to give my full stomach some room to settle, suddenly grateful that I don't have Mum cooking for me everyday. As much as it's the best meal I've had in a long time, if I was eating like this three times a day—which would definitely be the case if I still lived here—I'd spend most of my life fighting a food coma.

My phone starts to vibrate in my pocket and I shift in the seat so I can pull it out without having to stand up. Alyssa's name on the screen has me quickly straightening. We'd chatted a couple of times since I'd been in Quilpie and she sounded okay, but she hadn't really told me much about what she'd been doing. She'd mainly asked about everyone here which infuriated me when I was concerned about her. After all, she's the one still coming to terms with the loss of her mate.

"Lyss. Is everything okay?"

"Yes. I was ringing to see how you are? I couldn't help but notice a couple of new strands were added to the pride bonds and one was a little worked up not long ago. It had me a little worried." The concern is clear in the shaking of her voice.

"I'm sorry I didn't discuss the new members with you before th—"

"Jared, I trust your judgement," she says cutting me off. "I was just worried that one of my pride mates was upset and I couldn't be there for them. I tried to sit on it, but didn't last long before the need to call won out."

My heart stutters in my chest. "Is this hurting you? It was never my intention—"

"Jared!" She snaps down the phone once again cutting my apology short. Theo's eyes lock onto mine and I can see my concerns mirrored in them. "I. Am. Fine. If you don't trust my words, feel the bonds."

As much as I want to take her word for it, I can't. She's been so fragile for such a long time. I need to feel it. So focusing on the bonds deep inside me, I find the strand that leads to Alyssa and as I follow it, I'm filled with…ease. She's at ease.

I release a heavy breath as a weight lifts off my shoulders and I finally think that she's going to be okay. She may have lost her mate but she's no longer in danger of giving up on living and that is a huge breakthrough. Part of me wonders what could have caused her change but that's something I'll worry about when I arrive back in Mount Roxby. Perhaps it's just her alone time with Lee that has given her a new lease on life.

"See? I'm okay."

"You are." The words catch in my throat as I'm overcome with emotions. I've wanted nothing more than this since the day she lost Wes and to have that now, after we've just defeated another enemy, feels like a blessing.

Saskia strokes my back and I give her a grateful smile.

"See you soon Jared. I'm looking forward to welcoming

your mate and our new member to the pride." The line goes silent as she ends the call and I glance around the table to see a number of wet eyes.

They'd all heard the conversation—having supernatural hearing—and they all love and care for Alyssa so to know that she's finally going to be okay is a relief to them just as much as it is to me.

26

STORMY ARRIVAL

JARED PULLS UP on the drive of a house I've seen once before. A house that, at the time, I never imagined I'd return to.

As he turns off the engine he glances at the backseat and the sleeping child curled against the window. She'd been asleep for the last four hours, clearly exhausted from recent events. "I'm glad she finally got some real sleep."

"It'll only get better once she settles here." I smile, knowing what I say is the truth.

He nods in agreement. "Shall we?" he asks as he gestures towards the house. Not waiting for my reply he reaches for his door handle.

Placing my hand on his forearm I stop him. "Wait."

He turns his attention to me but doesn't say anything. Instead he waits for me to go on.

"Alyssa and you…" The second I start I regret it, unable to even bring myself to finish the question. It's such a jealous and petty question. If anything was between him and Alyssa I wasn't in the picture back then. It would be irrelevant now anyway because his lion chose me as his mate, but some little part of me needs to know the truth regardless.

"Alyssa is part of my pride. She was put in my protection out of trust from her alpha. There has never been anything more than alpha and a suffering pride member between us." He frowns. "If I had ever even thought of being more with her, I would have been taking advantage. She didn't need a lover, she needed a protector."

I knew what he was saying was the truth. I knew it before he'd even said it because Jared doesn't have it in him to take advantage of someone in such a dark place. Hell, he doesn't have it in him to take advantage of anyone, and that's one of the reasons I love him.

"I'm sorry I asked. I had no right—"

Reaching out, Jared slides his fingers over my cheek to cup one half of my face. "You have every right to ask. I wouldn't want you living with a question like that niggling away at you. I want you to be happy here and if you had worries like that you wouldn't be."

I release a breath and feel unexpectedly lighter. "I love you."

His smile widens and by the way his shoulders relax I can see that he loses the tension he'd been holding there. "I love you too."

His lips brush against mine in a chaste kiss and he tucks my loose hair behind my ear as his eyes lock onto mine. "Now are you ready to go and make this your home?"

I offer him a smile as my heart feels so full of love it could burst. "My home is wherever you are."

Love flows through our mating bond and he gives me a warm smile. "You go ahead, let yourself in. Alyssa is expecting us. I'll wake Maze and bring the bags in."

After giving him one last soft kiss, I slide out of the car and head for the front door. The door opens before I even reach the handle and I suddenly find myself suffocating in a mass of red curls.

"Saskia, welcome home. It's so good to see you again. I'm so happy that Jared has found his mate and that it's you. My wolf admired your strength the first time we met and that is exactly the kind of mate Jared and his lion needs," Alyssa says, her words coming so fast I can barely keep up.

As she pauses for a breath I quickly jump in hoping to calm her rambling down. "It's nice to see you again too, Alyssa."

A baby's cry fills the air and I step back trying to break her hold on me, completely expecting her to go to the baby. When she only squeezes me tighter I frown. "Isn't that Lee?"

"Oh yes." She finally releases me and waves a hand dismissively in the air. "He's fine. There's someone looking after him." And just like that his cries quieten down to a gentle happy cooing. "Come on in." She grabs my hand and pulls me into the house giving me no room to argue.

"How is everyone after the fight? It was so hard being so far away when I felt Jared get hit." She gives me a gives me a look that I can only guess is sympathy as she comes to a stop in in the lounge area. "You'll have felt worse and you were there with him. And then he got stronger and you got weaker. I didn't think my heart could take it. I'm so glad you're both safe and well."

Hearing Jared chatting to Maze we both turn to watch them enter.

Jared's eyes connect with mine, his lips turned up into a smile and his eyes sparkling with laughter at whatever Maze is telling him. He places his bags on the floor and heads towards us. I expect him to pull Alyssa into a hug straight-away so I'm surprised as he slides his hand into my hair and presses a kiss to my forehead as he passes. I relax at the loving gesture.

"Hey Lyss," he starts as he wraps her up in his arms. "You do look…better." He holds her at arms length, taking her in. I weigh her up and realise he's right. She looks so much brighter than she had when we'd left.

"I kept telling you I was okay. You wouldn't have had to

worry as much as you did if you'd have just taken my word for it." She shrugs as she steps out of his hold, her eyes falling on Maze. "And this must be our other new pride mate."

Jared steps out of the way and gestures for Maze to move closer. "This is Maze. Maze, this is Alyssa."

Alyssa stays where she is, clearly aware of Maze's apprehension which she'd be able to feel through the bonds just as much as I can. "It's nice to meet you Maze. I look forward to becoming friends with you."

Maze offers Alyssa a wave and a smile but nothing more. Having seen her with others I'm sure she'll warm up to Alyssa within a couple of hours. She knows Jared wouldn't allow anyone who would harm her within reach, but she still needs to observe them for a little while first to give them her full trust. Considering all she's been through, even that is amazing.

Jared's eyes roam over the rest of the room, a frown forming between his brows. "Where's my little man?"

A tall guy with warm brown skin and a short military style haircut, dressed in sweats and nothing more, brings baby Lee—who is cooing at the ceiling—cradled in his arm, into the room, coming from the hallway that I can only assume leads to the bedrooms. "He's right here, and more than ready for a feed."

Jared's alpha energy flows over my skin, leaving a sting behind, as he stares at the stranger with narrowed eyes. "Who the fuck are you?" The anger in his voice has my lioness on edge and, going by the mixed energy that suddenly fills the room, my animal isn't the only one reacting.

Turn the page to read an excerpt of **Everlasting Love**, *book 5* in the Mount Roxby series.

Coming in Late 2020

TRICK PLAY

I DROP onto the sofa as Ruby vanishes into thin air, grateful for the fact that she can't stick around during the day. I know she's only trying to be there for me but she's been overbearing, hovering over me every minute and trying to make me happy. Jared at least gives me space to just be, not pushing me to feel something I don't.

Within minutes my phone rings and, expecting it to be Jared checking in on me again—since he'd been doing it every couple of hours—I pick it up without looking at the screen. "You can feel me, surely you don't need to check in again so soon."

"I can't feel you anymore Lyss." Theo's words and the pain I could hear behind them cause my heart to hurt, like someone's squeezing it. A tear trails down my cheek as the thought makes me think of Wes's death, since that was exactly what happened to him.

"I'm sorry…" I start, unable to finish the sentence because I just don't have the words. He was my alpha, wanting nothing more than to protect and comfort me, and I all but threw him away. Replacing him with Jared.

"Lyss, you don't need to apologise for anything. You needed to be away from the pack and thankfully Jared was there to step in and be exactly what you required. I don't blame you for anything. I promise."

I swallow back the lump in my throat. "I still feel bad."

"Well you shouldn't. I love and miss you. And so do many of the pack members. But we all understand."

Theo's insistence eases something in my chest and I breathe a little easier. "Thanks Theo. I do miss you guys too. It's just…"

"We know," he says. "Anyway, I rang because I have an old friend coming to town tomorrow. The only problem is there's nowhere for him to stay, and I thought with Jared out of town he could maybe take his room for a few nights."

I frown. "You have plenty of spare rooms at your place."

"Yes. But he's not a wolf; in fact, he's kind of endangered and feels safer lying low." Theo is quick to answer and although his reasoning seems odd, it does sound genuine if not a little too rehearsed

"It's fine by me." I start. "It's a pack safe house after all, so any guest of yours is welcome. Jared would agree."

"Thanks. There's one other favour I need. Would you be able to pick him up from the bus station tomorrow at eleven?" I sigh and his supernatural hearing picks it up because he quickly forges on. "I'd go myself but Bel has some surprise planned and she won't let me out of it."

I know the surprise and it's a good one. She's coming to pick up Lee at eight and they are having him until lunchtime. Theo misses Wes a lot too, and to be able to spend time with Lee, who is a part of Wes, will help him heal and deal with his own grief. After all, that's what's happening with me. I'm healing more and more each day and that's mainly because I have Lee in my life.

As much I don't want to do it and know I don't have to, after all he isn't my alpha anymore and I'm not bound to do things he asks of me, I care for him and still want to help him out if I can. And it's not going to hurt me to drive into town and meet the guy. "Alright. I'll be there at eleven. Who should I be looking for?"

"You're a lifesaver. Thank you. He said he'd be wearing an ACDC shirt."

"Lets hope that he's the only one." I let out a soft giggle as I imagine a dozen people standing around the bus station all wearing ACDC shirts. After all, it's still a fairly popular band.

I eye the clock hanging on the wall above the TV as I place my phone on the arm of the chair. Lee will be up for a feed in two hours and I can't help but wonder if it's even worth going to bed. If I close my eyes right here and now I'm likely to fall asleep quicker than I am if I start moving around and getting ready for bed.

Choosing the chair, I curl my feet under me and snuggle into the plush cushions as I close my eyes.

Lee's hungry cries pierce the silence and I immediately open my eyes. The room is bright and for a moment I think it's because the light was on when I fell asleep. Only as I glance at the clock and see the time do I realise Lee slept through the night. It's six in the morning.

Jumping up, I dash into the bedroom wanting to ease my baby's cries and tell him thank you for letting me sleep through for the first time.

———

WALKING down Main Street my eyes fall on a loved up couple cooing over a baby stroller and I can't ignore the pang the sight sends through my heart. That would have been Wes and I. He'd be pouring all his love on Lee—he had a lot of love to give—and giving him adoring looks.

I step down the curb and stride across the road towards

the bus station. My ears are suddenly assaulted with the blaring of a car horn. Multiple horns.

Strong fingers wrap around my wrist and pull me back on to the pavement and head first into a hard body. The energy around us crackles and I'm more than certain he's a shifter because my energy isn't the only one running over my skin. I've never felt a reaction of energy like this from a clash of bodies.

The guy inhales deeply clearly taking in my scent. "Alyssa?"

My name coming off his lips startles me and I look at him with wide eyes as my wolf's ears perk up in interest. "Yes. How…"

"I think you're meant to be meeting me. I'm Doyle." He looks down at his hand, which is still wrapped around my wrist and he quickly releases me.

I take a quick step back suddenly needing some space between us. "How did you know my name?"

"Theo told me who I should be looking for when I spoke to him a couple of days ago."

I laugh and roll my eyes. "Funny that, when I only said I'd come late last night."

"Ah. Theo is still as sneaky as ever then."

I inhale in annoyance at Theo's tactics, suddenly wishing I'd thrown a spanner in the works and said no to the favour. Doyle's scent hits me and I'm taken aback, somewhat slightly confused. Theo had said he wasn't a wolf but I'd expected to be able to recognise his animal when I met him.

I frown. "What are you? I smell smoke…" I inhale again. "And roasted chestnuts. You remind me of Christmas."

He lets out a booming laugh and a number of passers-by glance in our direction. He leans forward. "I'm a dragon," he admits in a whispered voice.

"*Impossible.* There's none left."

Holding his hand between us he quickly shifts his fingers enough for me to catch a glimpse of his iridescent scales.

"Holy shit." I stare at him and know that I have a look of awe plastered on my face but I can't seem to wipe it off. It's not everyday you meet a dragon.

ACKNOWLEDGMENTS

To *the readers* that have stuck with me and waited patiently as I've written Jared's story. Thank you. YOU are who keeps me going on the hard days.

Sara Cartwright, thank you for coming up with Mazikeen's name and animal. I loved your idea of a Tazmanian Tiger.

Sam Destiny, you've waited so long for your man's story. I hope Jared and Sassy are all you hoped them to be.

Anna Crosswell from Cover Couture, when I saw this premade cover I knew it had to be Jared's Girl. I love your work and you were so easy to work with. Thank you for wrapping up my story in such a pretty package.

Jane from Tiny Tiger Edits, thank you for cleaning up my mess of extra commas and jumbled words.

ABOUT THE AUTHOR

Aimie Jennison is a Yorkshire lass living in Australia. She is a mother to three boisterous boys, two of which are teenagers who drive her crazy on a daily basis.

Aimie loves to people watch, it's her favourite way to come up with new characters and stories. So next time a stranger is staring at you in the street, don't panic, they could be an author basing a character on you.

Aimie has always loved to read and write. Paranormal, gay romance and crime/thrillers being her favourite genres. Her characters talk the loudest when she's at the beach or climbing a mountain.

Aimie would love to hear from you so don't shy away from contacting her.

For more information:
www.aimiejennison.com
aimiejennison@gmail.com

facebook.com/AuthorAimieJennison

twitter.com/Aim4theNeck

instagram.com/aim4theneck

amazon.com/author/Aimie-Jennison

bookbub.com/profile/aimie-jennison

goodreads.com/Aim4theNeck

pinterest.com/aim4theneck

Mount Roxby Series

Pride to Pack

Forever Young and Beautiful

Reclaiming the One

Love of Three

Mount Roxby Boxset

Mount Roxby: Book 1-3

Rossi Pack Series

Releasing the Wolf

Contemporary Romance

A Knight on the Titanic: A Short Story Inspired by the RMS Titanic